REVENGE IN THE CAPITOL

B. IVY WOODS

BRETAGEY PRESS

For my husband.

Thank you for supporting my dreams.

R achelle "Rae" Carter knew that she complained about D.C.'s humid summers, but she'd do almost anything to bring some of that heat to warm up her frigid hands right now. Thankfully, she was only several feet from her destination and almost sprinted to its front door. Once she was inside, she briefly waved at John, the owner of the Green Hat, before she spotted the people she came to meet.

"Long time, no see."

"I know, I know." Rae shook off her winter coat and placed it on a chair at the table. "You know how wild things have been."

Rae was meeting up with her three best friends at their usual hangout, the Green Hat. The foursome had discovered the place one summer and continued coming there ever since. They had even made friends with the owner of the bar.

"How are things going?" Evelyn "Eve" Jackson asked, turning her body toward Rae.

"They are going," Rae replied, flipping her dark brown

ponytail over her shoulder. She shivered briefly as her body tried to adjust to the temperature in the bar. She was thankful for the red sweater and blue denim jeans she wore out for this occasion.

The Green Hat's atmosphere was just what Rae was looking for this evening. Not much had changed since she and her friends found the bar years ago. The eighties power ballad that was playing from the speakers made her feel at home. The dive bar in DuPont Circle still had a laid-back vibe with posters on the walls from popular eighties and nineties bands. Patrons were playing darts and pool, but the dance floor and DJ booth were empty. She figured at some point everyone would migrate over there as the night went on.

"Well, do we need to pull the words out of you or what? What's going on? You've been cryptic in your texts this week." Olivia "Liv" Nicholls was never one to hold back what she was thinking.

"Ladies, I don't know. Things have just been stressful with Flint running for Congress and me trying to keep up with his new schedule and maintain my own with my job and my hobbies. It's just been one thing after the other, and I've had a hard time balancing it, that's all." Rae sighed as she started playing with the ends of her ponytail. "Sometimes, I swear I don't sleep. At least it feels that way.

"That makes sense. If it's any consolation, you never look stressed during any of the events I've seen you attend. In fact, I was starting to worry since you seemed too put together if that makes sense? Especially because I know you have been so busy lately. I mean, that's a compliment." Juliana "Jules"

Cartwright patted Rae's hand before returning her hand to her phone.

"Thanks," Rae said as she took a sip from the glass of red wine that someone at the table had ordered for her. Never had she been more grateful for someone to make a choice for her.

"So give us the 411. What's life like on the campaign trail?"

"I haven't heard anyone say 'the 411' in years, Eve. Way to date yourself." Eve rolled her eyes at Liv's comment and gestured for Rae to continue. "It's not what I thought it would be, to be honest. Like, I knew it would be hard, and I appreciate all the work that everyone is putting into the campaign. I'm ecstatic to be helping Flint. But I'd be lying if I said that it wasn't taking a toll. Physically and emotionally."

Jules turned toward Rae and said, "The physical toll that this would take on you or anyone makes sense. I guess I never considered the emotional toll it could have."

Rae nodded. "Now this isn't to say that being Flint's partner in all of this sucks. It...just made things harder. For example, I barely see him, and when I do, it's because I'm attending an event with him or his campaign is hosting an event, and I'm there meeting people and putting my best foot forward for the campaign. So, we don't go on dates much, and when I do get to see him alone, it's late at night when we're both exhausted. We might watch one show, and then it's time to go to bed. Then the next day, the same thing happens all over again. Sometimes we might have a day or two to ourselves, which is lovely. But other than that..." Rae trailed off before shrugging her shoulders.

"Have you talked to Flint about this?" Liv's question led Rae to glance at her before staring down at her drink.

"I have, and I think he's regretful, but what can he do? His team has jam-packed his schedule since he became the favorite to win the primary in June."

"Does he have to attend every event? I know my dad attended a lot of events on behalf of our foundation, but my mom asked him to slow down because he was getting older, and he had a capable staff that could carry the load. He did, but I know that this is different for Flint because he is trying to get elected, so he needs to be out and mingling with the public."

"And I know this is his dream, and I accept that right now, things will be hectic. I just don't like that they are."

"Fair," Liv said before taking a sip from her beer.

"Do you think it would be worth having another conversation with him? I understand that he has to attend these events, but maybe he could take an evening or Saturday or Sunday off and spend it with you? It doesn't even have to be one day a week. Maybe one day every two weeks? It shouldn't hurt his campaign. Plus, it might also give both of you an opportunity to recharge from the stress that has to be developing from all of this."

Rae tossed that idea back and forth in her head and realized Eve was right. Why couldn't Flint take a day or two off per month and spend it with her? Even if it meant date night at home, it would still give them some time to spend together, which she wanted.

"Yeah, that's an excellent idea." Rae offered Eve a smile before taking another sip of her wine. "He's planning on coming over tonight, so I'll talk to him about it then. If he doesn't fall asleep, that is. How's everything going with y'all?"

It surprised Rae when she didn't hear groans from the

group. Liv and Jules shook their heads before Eve responded, "I wanted to ask you something."

"Shoot."

"Would you mind if I do a profile on you and Flint? This isn't official or anything, and I would never want to cash in on our friendship, but I thought it would be an outstanding opportunity."

Rae was silent for a moment. "I could ask Flint what he thinks. I would also need to clear it with my job." Rae hesitated again before she said, "What did you have in mind? Would people think you're being biased with this profile? I'm not sure how this would work."

"Maybe something like a day in the life? I imagine it must be complicated because he's not only focused on his campaign goals, but how to balance them with his personal life." Eve realized what she said and held her hands up. "I don't mean a tell-all of your business, though. We can figure out how to make it work if you both want to do it."

Rae looked at the ceiling as she tried to think about the possibilities. Her eyes floated back down, and she focused her attention on Eve. "I don't see how it could hurt. Let's see what Flint and his team have to say about it." Rae held up her glass to clink it with Eve's. Then Jules and Liv joined in before the group took a sip.

Rae cleared her throat. "I just realized how much of a toll this has been taking on me mentally too. I've been second-guessing myself a lot more now. The outfits I wear, what I look like when I head to barre class, the suggestions I make at work." Flint's congressional race had gotten national attention given how close the race was to D.C., and this being the first time this congressional seat had been open in twenty-five years.

"I'd be a nervous wreck if my significant other or I was in the spotlight. Do you know how much stuff could be dug up on me? Whew, call a tabloid. Right. Now." Liv emphasized the last two words by banging her hand on the table. Rae, who had been drinking her wine, snorted and coughed. She snatched a napkin off the table and covered her mouth. Eve reached over to help her friend clear her throat. Once she stopped coughing, she glanced around the bar to see if anyone noticed her snafu, but no one had.

"Yeah, you're a little paranoid, girl." Eve stopped patting Rae on the back.

"I know, I just...don't want to do anything that jeopardizes Flint's chances to get the seat. Now, there's a chance he won't win, but I don't want to be the cause."

"Fair, but don't change yourself to fit into a mold that you believe the public wants you to be in. It's not fair to you because you shouldn't have to change yourself for anyone, and you didn't ask for this attention."

And there were the wise words from Eve that Rae, most of the time, didn't know she needed. "You're right. Thanks."

"I think I can speak for everyone by saying if there is any way that any of us can help, let us know." Jules smiled while Liv snorted.

"Speak for yourself." She paused a beat before continuing, "You know I'm kidding. We're always there for you. No matter what."

Rae let her grin take over her face. "Well, would you guys be game for attending or volunteering at some of these events with me?"

"Do we get special privileges? Like a friend of the candidate gets some pretzels in between answering phones or stuffing envelopes?"

Rae rolled her eyes at the look on Liv's face.

"Anything for you, Your Majesty." Rae turned to Eve and Jules and said, "We just won't tell her that snacks and beverages will already be offered."

"I heard that."

"And that was the point," said Rae in a singsong voice. "I'll let you know what the campaign has planned. Plus, who knows? Maybe Kane will attend or host a fundraiser on behalf of Homes for Vets." Rae hoped her pointed look at Eve conveyed everything she was trying to say.

Eve gave her a one-finger salute before she said, "I don't know why you're looking at me."

"Oh, you know why I'm looking at you."

Rae watched as Jules looked at her, then at Eve, and then back at her. "Am I missing something here?"

"Eve, why don't you explain what Jules is missing?" Rae leaned toward Eve and rested her head on her fist as the corners of her lips tipped up.

"I would if I had any idea what you were talking about."

Rae slowly turned toward Jules and said, "So since Eve won't come clean, I'll spill what I know, which to be fair, isn't much. When Kane came to help me move, she froze like a deer in headlights, and whenever she's been around him since then, she's had the same reaction. Also, it doesn't help that Kane couldn't take his eyes off of her while we were moving my stuff into my new apartment and at several other events we've all attended together."

"Still don't understand what you're talking about."

"Is that the answer you're going to stick with?"

"Uh-huh."

Rae glared at Eve before shrugging her shoulders. "You know we'll all find out what happened one way or another."

It was Eve's turn to shrug as she gulped down her drink.

"Uh-huh, my ass."

Rae's comment caused Jules to chuckle. "I'm just going to change the subject. Our foundation has already reached out to Flint's campaign, but I wanted you to know if they wanted us to host a fundraiser or take part in one that is already in the works, we'd be happy to do it. It wouldn't be for as much money as it would be if he were the official nominee, but we can contribute something."

Rae watched as Jules glanced at the other women before she turned her attention back to her. "But this isn't something we need to talk about now. Just figured I would let you know before I forget."

Rae forced a smile on her face. "Sounds good."

With that, Liv started talking about her latest dates, and Rae tried everything in her power to focus on what was coming out of her friends' mouths. She slipped in and out of a daydream as she thought about how her life had changed since Flint's campaign began. She never thought in a million years that she would spend a lot of her time thinking about Flint's schedule instead of her own. And to her, that was troubling.

2

R ae got home and took off her shoes near the door. She hung up her coat and strolled into her living room. Snatching her phone from her purse, she tossed the bag onto the couch as she made her way into her kitchen. She figured hydrating after an evening out with her friends should be high on her priority list. Grabbing a glass from her cabinet, she walked over to her fridge to fill her cup with water. While sipping her water, she turned her phone's alerts back on and checked her messages to see what she'd missed.

Flint: I miss you.

He had texted her while she was in the cab back to her apartment. Rae reread the message several times before replying.

Rae: Miss you too. Will you be coming over soon?

She was happy to see the three dots that indicated Flint was responding right away.

Flint: Yep. This event is wrapping up soon. Hopefully will be headed toward you in 30.

Rae: *Sounds good. See you soon.*

Rae drank some more of the water before walking back into the hallway. She headed into her bedroom and placed the glass down on her dresser. She took another look at her phone and realized that she, depending on where Flint was, still had at least another forty-five minutes before he arrived. Wanting to take full advantage of the time, she jumped into the shower to remove the grime and stress of the day.

She took a deep breath as the water rolled off her shower cap and back in waves. The tension in her shoulders was still there, but the shower and the soft floral lavender scent from her body wash relaxed her.

Her quick ten-minute shower turned into a twenty-minute one, but there were no regrets. When she finished drying off, moisturizing, and putting on a pair of yoga pants and a college sweatshirt, she retreated to her living room to wait for Flint. She turned the television on and checked her messages once again to see if Flint had updated her, but he hadn't.

Mindlessly, she kept her eyes on the television and her phone as she waited. Her waiting turned into daydreams before her phone pinged, letting her know there was a message.

Flint: *I'm here.*

Her heart swelled as she walked to her front door. She swung it open before Flint could knock. Rae wasn't sure who moved first, but when she felt his arms around her, everything felt right, and that's all she wanted.

"How'd your day go?"

"Not too bad. Busy as usual. Thanks," Flint said as he

raised the glass of water that Rae had just placed in front of him. She sat down on the couch beside him and snuggled up against him as he wrapped his arm around her. "How was your day?"

"Not too bad. Went to happy hour with the girls."

"Oh, that's right, that was tonight. How'd that go? How are they?" Flint placed the glass of water down and picked up his phone after his ringtone went off.

"It went well. It was nice seeing them in person instead of chatting on the phone." Rae stared at Flint when he didn't respond to her. He looked to be responding to an email on his phone. A few moments later, she cleared her throat to get his attention.

"Ah—sorry. Rick sent me an email, and I thought I could respond quickly. I apologize. What were you talking about?" Flint paused before answering his own question. "Happy hour with the girls."

Rae debated saying anything about him ignoring her, but decided against it. "Yes. In fact, Eve mentioned maybe doing a profile on you, the campaign, and me if that was something you were interested in."

Flint thought about it for a second before he said, "That sounds like it could be a good idea. I'll run it by Rick." Rick Campbell was Flint's campaign manager, who had since become an integral part of their daily lives. He was excellent at his job and getting things done, in Rae's opinion, so she understood why Flint had hired him to run his campaign.

"Sounds good," Rae replied before she turned her body toward the television when Flint's phone went off again. Out of the corner of her eye, she could see Flint reaching for his phone before placing his hand back down on his lap. When he did it a second time, Rae sighed. "You can pick up your phone."

"But I don't want to interrupt—"

"It's fine."

"It's never fine when you say 'it's fine.'"

He wasn't wrong. "True. I was just hoping it would just be you and me tonight. Not me, you, and Rick. Plus, I figured we would be heading to bed soon anyway."

Flint sighed. "You know what? You're right." He took his phone, turned the ringer off, and put it face down on the coffee table. "We don't spend much time alone together as it is. Seeing as how this wasn't super important, Rick can wait."

Rae saw the sincerity in his eyes and gave him a small smile. "Thank you," she whispered as she snuggled up against him again. She checked the time on her own phone before also putting her device face down on the coffee table. Flint mindlessly played with the soft, dark strands of her hair. "Are you tired? We could stay up for a bit and watch TV."

"I'm not tired," Flint said, just before a yawn escaped his lips. Rae giggled and shook her head.

"Yep, totally not tired. Why don't we head to bed and maybe plan to do something tomorrow evening? After your events? We haven't gone out to dinner in such a long time." Rae's eyes traveled from their resting place on Flint's chest up to his eyes. His chin, which had been sitting on the top of her head, moved, and his eyes were now staring into hers. "I think I can make that work. Have your people call my people."

The belly laugh that Rae released took her by surprise. It

also relieved the rest of the tension that she'd felt a few minutes before. "I needed that. Let's go to sleep and figure out our plans tomorrow morning." Rae stood up from the couch and started walking toward the bedroom before she felt Flint grasp her hands. She looked up at him as he gently pulled her toward him, and his gaze moved from her eyes to her lips.

"I didn't get a chance to kiss you earlier," he said as he leaned down toward her.

"That's true. How silly of me to forget," she whispered. She stood on her tiptoes to meet him halfway. When their lips met, the worries that Rae experienced flew out of her mind as her main goal was to get even closer to Flint. She didn't know how long they spent kissing, but when the kiss ended, they were both breathing heavily.

"Are you sure that we can't do something else besides go to bed to sleep? Anything else?"

His questions made Rae chuckle as she started walking toward the bedroom. "Positive."

Soft, light touches on her skin aroused Rae from her peaceful slumber. She smiled before whispering, "Good morning."

"Good morning, beautiful."

Rae opened her eyes and found a smiling Flint sitting next to her on the bed. In his hand was a mug of steaming hot coffee.

"For you, milady." He handed her the mug.

"Thank you, kind sir." She took a sip from her coffee and

closed her eyes. The smell of freshly made coffee always helped awaken her senses, let alone having a sip of it. When she opened her eyes, she saw that he had his own mug in his hand.

"Well, this was a nice surprise. Are you getting ready to head out soon?"

Flint nodded. "What are you up to today?"

Rae thought about her schedule for a moment. "Honestly, nothing. My plan was to go to a barre class and then spend the rest of the day cleaning and organizing. Maybe even try to do a little bit of work that I wasn't able to finish this week. Why?"

"You mentioned going out to dinner last night, and I want to make that happen. So how about I pick you up at six? It'll be low-key, so you don't have to worry about being 'on.'"

Rae caught the subtle comment. Since Flint's run for Congress, they both felt that they always had to be extremely proper to the point that it was a bit suffocating. The fear of making a mistake was somewhat anxiety-inducing for Rae. "That sounds like an excellent plan." She placed a small kiss on his lips as she tried to make sure she didn't hit his mug with her own nor spill her coffee onto the bedsheets. She broke the kiss and chuckled when he tried to deepen it. "Are you headed out now? I can make breakfast."

"I have a breakfast meeting in about forty-five minutes, so I probably have enough time to finish this coffee and jump into the shower." Flint took another sip of the coffee before putting the mug down and heading over to her dresser. He opened one of the drawers and took out some clothes for himself. He and Rae each had a drawer at each other's apartments when they realized how much of a pain it was to have to get up and head home to change after they spent the night at the other's apartment. Rae looked up when Flint sat back on the bed and took another sip from his mug.

"I'm excited for tonight." Rae's words caused a smile to appear on his face. "Are you going to tell me where we're going?"

Flint shook his head. "Nope. That's for me to know and for you to see later."

"Well, then are you going to tell me the dress code?"

"Sure. I'll tell you later."

"Wait—what?"

"I'll tell you later. I did already give you a hint. Everything is low-key." Flint gulped down the rest of the coffee and stood up.

Rae wanted to point out that they could still be low-key while dressed up. "Flint, you know I hate surprises, and now you won't even tell me what I should wear?"

Flint placed the mug on her bedside table before leaning down to look her right in the eyes.

"There was a time when you liked my surprises. Like the time we went kayaking when we first started dating. Or when we sent each other photos of—"

"Okay. Okay. That's enough of that." Rae hoped he wouldn't bring up any memories of *those* photos.

"Just trust me, okay? We're going to have a great time."

"Fine. As long as you give me enough time to figure out what to wear."

Flint gave her another kiss on the lips before standing up to his full height. He strolled toward the bathroom before tossing over his shoulder, "I'll tell you five minutes before six."

It took everything in Rae not to throw a pillow at his retreating frame as she chuckled at his response.

3
———

Rae stood back to admire her handiwork after she finished cleaning her stove. Flint had been gone for a few hours, and she went to barre class and came home and showered. Then, she started a load of laundry and dishes, which led to her continuing to clean the kitchen.

She walked over to her sink and took off the gloves she was using to protect her hands. Once she finished washing her hands, she dried them off and walked across the room to the fridge to grab a soda. Then she walked into the living room and grabbed her phone off of the coffee table. Seeing no new messages after the ones from her friends, confirming that they all made it home, she texted them to catch up.

Rae: Drank too much at happy hour?

Eve: Yep.

Liv: Don't even ask.

Jules: I'm doing great, thanks for asking.

Rae smiled at Jules's response. She wasn't shocked that Jules was doing better than Eve and Liv, even though it was late morning. Almost afternoon. Jules usually woke up early and paced herself better than everyone else, so her being chipper made sense.

Rae: *Guess that tequila hit back.*

She chuckled at her comment before putting her phone back down on the table in front of her. Rae stood back up to continue tidying the kitchen when her phone buzzed. She picked it up and grinned when she saw the message.

Flint: *I love you.*

Rae: *I love you too.*

That short message put more pep in her step as she continued to clean her apartment.

At about four o'clock, Rae was finishing folding up her laundry when her phone's ringtone played. She grabbed her phone and swiped over to her text messages.

Flint: *Check your front door.*

Rae stared at the message but didn't move.

"You have to be outside your mind if you think—" Rae's mumblings stopped when her ringtone played again.

Flint: *I'm not trying to prank you. Check your front door.*

Rae stared at the offending object because she was annoyed at how well Flint knew her. With a huff, she stood up and walked over to her front door. She looked through the peephole and saw a white box sitting on her doorstep. Taking a deep breath and vowing to come back and haunt Flint if she died, she opened the front door and stared at the box. Feeling foolish for having stared at the box for longer than necessary, she bent down and picked it up. She shook the box as she tried to figure out what Flint could have sent her. She placed it on the dining room table and grabbed her phone.

Rae: *What did you send me?*

The white box was medium-sized, but when she shook it, the contents seemed smaller. The return address didn't give away what was inside, either. Rae ignored her ringtone as it played again because she figured it was Flint telling her to open the box instead of asking him twenty questions. She walked into her kitchen and grabbed a pair of scissors before heading back into the dining room to complete her mission. Rae opened the box and was greeted with an envelope titled "Open Me First" and another box. However, this box was white and flatter than the first one. Figuring she should continue following directions, she opened the envelope first and read the card.

Rae,

I saw this and immediately thought of you. Our date night is casual, but I would love it if you wore this with whatever you picked out. I know you hate surprises, but I'm happy to have the chance to spoil and spend time with you tonight. See you soon.

Love,

Flint

She reread the card before placing it on the table and moved to open the second box. Her heart thundered outside of her chest as she stared at the small white box in front of her. This could definitely be a piece of jewelry. She reined in her thoughts because the box was too long to contain an engagement ring, and Flint wasn't there.

Rae opened the smaller white box and moved the wrapping paper. She stared in amazement at the sight in front of her. In the box sat a beautiful gold necklace. The necklace was an infinity symbol intertwined with a heart, and the jeweler had made both of diamonds. She put together an outfit in her mind as she gathered the necklace and sent off a quick text to Flint before dashing into her bedroom.

Rae: *Thanks for the sweet note and the necklace. I'll see you soon.*

A few minutes before six, Rae checked herself in the mirror to see if there was anything she should change about her look. She tossed one of her curls over her shoulder as she put the brown thick-heeled boots she'd selected on her feet. The boots accentuated Rae's denim-covered legs, and she finished the outfit with a red sweater, gold earrings and bracelet, and a nude purse. As she was spritzing a light, floral perfume on herself, she heard a knock on her front door. She double-checked her phone to make sure that Flint hadn't sent a message. Seeing none, she checked the peephole before answering. An enormous smile formed on her face as she opened the door.

"I was expecting a text to let me know that you were here."

"I like to keep you on your toes. You look stunning, and that necklace was definitely the right choice." Flint's fingers grazed along her skin as he touched the necklace that was resting just above her chest, and Rae's breath hitched. When she looked into his eyes, he was looking back at her, and she knew they were sharing the same thoughts. He cleared his throat and dropped the necklace before handing her the purple flowers in his hand. Memories of the kayak date that they went on years ago flowed into her mind and made her smile. "Plus, I wanted to give you these now so you could put them in some water."

"Pulling out all the stops. Thanks so much for the flowers," Rae said as she strolled into her kitchen. She heard Flint close the door and follow her. "Are we in a rush? I can get these into some water within five minutes," Rae said as she placed the flowers on the counter.

"No rush. Reservations aren't until 6:45, and the restaurant is only about twenty minutes away."

"Great. Can you hand me a vase from that cabinet over there so I can put these away?"

Rae and Flint chatted as she set up the flowers the way she wanted to before they headed for the door. Once they were in Flint's sedan, the two made small talk about how the rest of their days went.

"So, you still won't tell me where we're going?"

Flint glanced at her and shot her a smirk. "Nope."

"Come on. We're almost there."

"Which is exactly why you can wait until we get there." Flint chuckled before glancing over at her again. "Did I tell you how stunning you look tonight?"

"You did, but I can always hear it again." She made a big show of flipping her loose curls over one shoulder, but some of her hair missed the memo and remained in their position.

"You look stunning. Took my breath away when you opened the door."

Rae smiled, brushing one of her dark brown curls behind her ear. "Thanks. And I didn't thank you for this beautiful necklace. Thank you. It was unexpected."

"Like I said, I like to keep you on your toes."

"How did you know this was something that I would like?"

Flint took a moment to answer due to him focusing on

driving once more. "I did my homework. Jules also helped me a bit. I thought about buying you the heels you've been talking about for two weeks now, but my mom used to tell me that if you buy someone a pair of shoes, then they'll walk out of your life." He glanced her way once more and put his hand on her knee. "I didn't want to risk that."

Rae made a mental note to thank Jules later and, at the same time, tried to keep her emotions together. Flint pulled up outside of what looked to be an office building in McLean, Virginia. A valet appeared as Flint turned off his car and opened his door. Before Rae could step out on her own, Flint was at her side helping her out of the car. Flint stepped around to chat with the valet while Rae wandered up to the front door of the office building. When Flint joined her and opened the door for her, she asked, "Where are we?"

"You'll see," he said with a smile as he led her into the building.

4

"I still can't believe you got us into Michael's. This restaurant only opened up a few months ago and was booked for months out. Supposedly. Had you been planning this for a while?" Rae took another bite of the lobster she had ordered while she waited for Flint's response. His reply took a little longer than normal because he was finishing a piece of his filet mignon.

"A friend from childhood pulled a few strings and got us in. I thought since things have been chaotic in our lives right now, that this would be a great date night."

"It probably helped that I have been bringing Michael's up at least once a week."

Flint chuckled. "Yes, that did help."

Although laughter could be heard in his words, the look he gave her when their eyes connected said so much more. Adoration. Affection, Appreciation. The mood in the restaurant topped everything off due to its low lights, smooth jazz and impeccable food. The company wasn't bad either.

"Do you remember when I came out to Denver and we

hung out at this really cool bar that was basically an arcade inside of a bar?"

Rae let the red wine she had just finished sipping, sit in her mouth for a beat before swallowing the drink.

"I do. I decimated you in Skee-Ball."

"You did not."

Rae sat back in her chair with a smirk. "I seem to remember our matches differently than you do."

"I have no idea what you're talking about."

Rae's body snapped forward, eyebrow raised. "Are you now claiming the matches didn't happen?"

Flint shrugged before taking a drink from his glass of water. Rae stared at him incredulously, which caused Flint to burst into laughter. By that point, Rae couldn't control her emotions either and joined him.

The couple enjoyed a lovely evening of not talking about anything related to the campaign. Rae had grown to crave the moments they had alone as much as a flower needs the sun. The couple was back in his car, and Rae looked back at the building with longing. This was the end of their beautiful night. Just as Flint was putting the car in drive, his phone rang. The. End.

"Well, at least your phone had no trouble connecting to the car's Bluetooth this time. And it's Rick," Rae said with a sigh.

"Hey, Rick. What's up?"

"I had a few things I wanted to run by you. Are you busy?"

"Just driving home after dinner with Rae."

"Ah. Hi, Rae."

"Hey, Rick. Hope everything is going well."

"Can't complain, can't complain." With that, Rick

launched into the things he needed to tell Flint. At first, Rae tried her best to listen in on the conversation, but as it went on, she paid more attention to her phone. She knew that the few things that Rick had to talk to Flint about would end up taking another hour or so. Her phone vibrating startled her.

Liv: *How is everyone doing?*

Rae: *Great. On our way back home. How about you?*

Liv: *Just finished folding laundry...and I'm proud to say it was right after I finished washing them. Where did you go?*

Rae: *To Michael's. Flint somehow got us reservations there for tonight.*

Jules: *That's fantastic, and I'm sure well needed. I'm doing good. Binge-watching a series.*

Rae: *You have no idea. We had a marvelous time.*

Rae looked out the window and watched the streetlights fly by as Flint drove to his apartment.

She zeroed in on her phone and typed out another message to the group chat.

Rae: *Flint is talking to Rick right now. I swear they talk with one another more than Flint and I do.*

Eve: *Doesn't that come with running a campaign, though?*

Eve was, of course, the voice of reason, but Rae didn't know how much she was in the mood to hear this reasoning.

Rae: *I get that, but I want just one night where Rick doesn't have to call Flint and interrupt our time together. I guess I'm...jealous? I don't know if that's the correct word to describe it.*

Jules: *It sounds like you miss how things were before Flint started campaigning.*

"I'll have to check in with Rae about that."

The sound of her name forced Rae to look up from her phone and turn to Flint. She tapped him on the knee, and when he looked at her, she mouthed *What?* Flint mouthed back, *Later*, which she assumed meant after he wrapped up his phone call with Rick. Rae turned her attention back to her group chat when Rick started talking about another topic.

Rae: *Without a doubt. Although we were coming off of all the drama that went down with the Hopkinses, which was a hot mess by itself, I feel like our attention wasn't being pulled in several directions like it is now.*

Liv: *Have you heard anything else about them?*

Rae: *Not much. I think I mentioned before that they and Gladys admitted to everything, but Gladys didn't know how far her friends had taken it. Jules might know more since her parents run in the same social circle as them. I have refused to ask Flint about it to avoid aggravating myself.*

Jules: *Haven't heard much about them, either. Neither Mom nor Dad has mentioned talking to them, but I'll ask. Haven't seen or heard much from Cassandra, either.*

"Rae." Once again, Rae looked up at the sound of her name being called. It was then she realized the car had stopped moving.

"Are we at your apartment?"

Flint nodded his head before giving her a hint of a smile. "I parked about a minute ago after hanging up with Rick, and you didn't move an inch."

"I guess I was into my phone. Sorry about that."

"And I'm sorry that Rick interrupted our drive home."

"I get it. It's campaign stuff. You need to communicate a lot."

"But it's getting between me spending quality time with you."

"It is. But it's also something I signed up for when we got back together."

Flint nodded his head before exiting the car. He swung around the hood and opened the door for Rae. They both walked through the lobby of his apartment building and waved at the person stationed at the front desk. After they rode the elevator up to Flint's floor, they entered his apartment and changed into their sweats.

The couple sat down on Flint's leather couch. Where Rae's apartment was designed with shades of lighter colors, Flint's apartment was a bit darker with rich browns, black, and white. Rae searched for the remote to the TV that hung across from the couch.

"What goals do you want to achieve, Rae?" Flint's question made Rae pause her search.

"Uh. Well, I want to get a promotion sometime within the next year or so. Whether that's with my current job or by finding a new one—"

Flint interrupted her. "I was thinking more about personal goals versus professional ones."

What do I want? Rae sat down but didn't respond for several moments. "That's a hard question. I think I've gotten so caught up in what was best for you and your campaign I haven't focused on what I want." She glanced at Flint and saw that he was nodding his head. He placed his hand over hers but said nothing.

A few more minutes went by before Rae spoke again.

"I want to travel more. Like, I loved going to Bermuda, even though I wasn't happy because of other circumstances," she said, alluding to the fight they had before she left for Bermuda with her friends a few months before.

"I must make that up to you." Rae bit down on her lip, but that couldn't stop the smile that was growing on her face. A vacation at some point sounded amazing, but with the campaign in full swing, it probably wouldn't be soon.

"Do you think after you win, it would be feasible to sneak away for a few days? Maybe in between the holidays?"

It was Flint's turn to smile. "I'm glad you're confident I will win, but we shall see about that. And sometime between the holidays sounds great. Maybe we could even have our families get together for the holidays. We're all in the same area."

That caused Rae to whip her head around to glare at Flint. "I don't know about that. I'm not over your mom attempting to orchestrate our breakup and then trying to force you to date Cassandra. You know, that entire scheme was a bit...much."

"Touché."

"Also, I'm not too sure how my mother will react to your mother. You were there when we told her the full story about who was sending me threatening messages."

"I know, I know. I was just throwing it out there."

"Understandable. Well, we have plenty of time before any of this would happen anyway, so let's see where we are in a few months."

"Makes sense." Flint stood up from his spot on the couch.

Rae looked at him, then at a photo in the room, then back at him. She opened her mouth to say something but closed it just as fast. She took a deep breath and said, "I want to have a family of my own at some point, too."

Rae watched as Flint turned to look at her over his shoulder before sitting back down on the couch. He scooted closer to Rae and placed his arm around her shoulders as she leaned into his body. She felt as if she had just bared her soul to him as she waited with bated breath for his response.

"I do, too," he whispered as he brushed a soft kiss onto her forehead. "This takes me back to when we talked about this the first time around."

"Yeah, it was during one of the weekends I flew out to visit you after you moved."

Rae smiled at the memory. "I miss that time in our lives. Things were complicated with you moving away, but it also seemed simpler because I think we have more obligations now. Not that serving your country isn't a tremendous deal or obligation because it is, but—"

Flint chuckled before he said, "I understand what you meant."

"And on top of that, you're running a campaign. It's intense."

"That it is. I want to help you achieve your goals." Rae felt another light kiss on her forehead before Flint cleared his throat. "I know you're giving up a lot to help with my dream. Thank you. I'll do the same for you. Let's make your dreams a reality."

His words caused her pulse to race as thoughts of what could be floated through her mind. The emotion in Flint's voice led Rae to look into eyes. He looked down at her, and she leaned over to give him a passionate kiss on the lips.

5

———

Rae woke to the sound of the shower running. It took her a few seconds to get her bearings and remember that she had slept over at Flint's house.

"Why are you up so early?" Rae asked herself as she scrambled to untangle herself from the warm cocoon she had woven herself into throughout the night. Once she was free, she got up, adjusted her pajamas, and headed toward the closed bathroom door. Her hands migrated up to her hair, and she rolled her eyes at the fact that she would have to tackle her hair in its current state. She knocked on the door and waited for a reply before she dashed into the bathroom and shut the door.

Flint peeped his head from around the door and gave her an enormous grin. "Good morning."

"How are you so chipper right now?" Rae growled as she made her way toward the bathroom counter. She turned around to glimpse Flint's silhouette behind the frosted-over shower door. Finding herself staring a few seconds longer than necessary, she turned her body toward the bathroom counter and found her toothbrush and toothpaste.

"Because you're here."

Rae shook her head as she brushed her teeth.

"Remember we were talking about what to do with the television in the bedroom?"

Rae said a muffled no as she spit in the sink.

"I was thinking it might be a good idea to hang the television on that dresser on the wall. That way, you'll have more room in our bedroom."

Rae stopped brushing her teeth for a second as she contemplated his words. She did a double-take as she watched her eyes widen in the bathroom mirror. *Did he just say our bedroom?*

"I mean, the decision is pretty much up to you, babe. This is your apartment." *There, that settled that.*

"But I want your opinion. Besides, you are probably here just as often as I am nowadays."

Rae mentally gave him that win because that wasn't a lie. She took her time answering as she continued washing up.

"If it's something you think you'll use, then go for it. It won't bother me." Rae paused a beat before changing the subject. "What time do you think you'll be home tonight?"

"Not sure, but I assume it will be late. I have at least two events tonight and possibly a third. Not counting the meetings I have earlier in the day. How about once I am done, I'll stop by your place, or you can meet me here?"

Rae stopped mid-lather. "Wait. What?"

Flint turned the shower off and opened the shower door. He reached out and grabbed the towel before pulling it into the shower with him. Rae watched him in the mirror and made circular motions on her face. She rinsed her face and patted it dry before she looked up again. There was Flint, standing in front of the shower with only a towel wrapped around his waist. Rae smirked as she studied his body, thoughts flying through her mind that made her want to forget all about getting ready for work.

"I was hoping you'd join me in the shower."

"I thought about it, but I showered last night."

"I know, but I still would have enjoyed the company."

"And we both would be late for work," Rae said. She took several steps forward until she was standing in front of Flint. "You probably should finish getting ready."

Flint's hand caressed her shoulder as he played with the strap of her tank top. When his finger brushed up against her skin, it took everything in her to not shiver. They didn't have time for this right now.

"I love you, but you need to go get ready, and I need to figure out what to do with my hair," she said with a smile.

"Okay, okay," Flint said as he leaned in and gave her a quick peck on the lips. He gave her a soft pat on the butt as he left the bathroom to finish getting dressed.

Although she longed for his touch, Rae turned around and walked back to the bathroom counter. She grabbed her toiletry bag and spent the next few minutes getting herself ready for work. Rae caught a glimpse of her reflection, but how she looked was the furthest thing from her mind. Flint wanted to move in together. Rae would have thought that his words would have made her ecstatic but here she was, trying to figure out why there was a small amount of worry there instead.

Many hours later, Rae stretched her arms as she took a break from staring at the computer screen. She checked the time on her laptop and noticed that it was 6:30 p.m. She stood up and started packing her bag to head home. Rae was trying to get her bearings when there was a knock on her door.

"Come in," she said as she placed her laptop into her bag.

Her boss, Danielle, peeked her head around the door and greeted Rae with a grin. "I'm surprised you're still here. It's late."

"I'm surprised too. One minute it was three, and then the next I knew, it was half past six."

"That happens sometimes. I was just checking in on you since I saw your light was still on. I can wait for you if you're heading out right now."

Rae nodded her head and said, "Yep. Was about to change into my flats, grab my coat, and then head on out." Once she was ready to go, she met Danielle at her door, and the two walked to the elevator.

"Everything going okay? Do you need any help with any of the projects you're working on?"

Rae took a moment to think but shook her head. "I think everything is going pretty well. Unless I've messed up somewhere?" She glanced at Danielle before pressing the button to summon the elevator to their floor.

"No. Your job performance has been exceptional, and if something was wrong, I would've mentioned it during our one on one. I just know things have been super busy here and with Flint's campaign ramping up. If you need help, just ask.

Sometimes it's hard for us as women to ask for help when we need it. For various reasons."

Danielle's comment caused Rae to pause. Before she could think of a response, the elevator doors opened, and the two stepped inside. Danielle leaned over and pressed the button for the lobby and then stepped back.

"Thanks for checking up on me."

"Of course." The pair made small talk as they rode down the elevator. Once they reached the lobby of their office building, the two waved as they headed off in separate directions. Although Rae tried to push work aside, Danielle's comment kept replaying in her head.

Rae arrived at Flint's apartment building and waved at the person at the front desk as she made her way to the elevator. Once the elevator arrived on Flint's floor, she walked to his door and typed in the passcode. She heard the door unlock, and she slipped inside. Rae flicked the light switch on and took off her coat. After hanging it in the front hall closet, she toed her shoes off, grabbed her purse, and walked into the living room. She placed her bag on his couch and took her phone out before heading into the kitchen. She immediately went to the cabinet that held some wineglasses that Flint had purchased on her behalf to make her feel more comfortable in his apartment. Rae smiled as she grabbed the wineglass and poured her favorite wine that had become a permanent fixture in his home.

Since he was running circles in her mind, she sent him a quick message to check up on him but was surprised to find she already had a message from him.

Flint: *How is everything going? Are you at the apartment?*

Rae: *Everything is fine. I'm drinking some wine in your* *apartment.*

She strolled back into the living room, wineglass and phone in hand, and set them down on his coffee table. Rae fished the remote out from between the cushions on the couch and got comfortable.

Flint: *Good. I don't know how long this last event will last, so I'm not sure what time I'll be there.*

After Rae read his last message, she laid her head back on the couch, closed her eyes, and sighed. A smirk slowly formed on her face. She grabbed her phone, unbuttoned the first few buttons of her shirt, and snapped a photo on her phone.

Rae: *Miss you.*

With that, the photo and the message were off to Flint's phone. She tossed her phone next to her on the couch, and it landed with the screen facing up.

Rae took another sip of her wine. She checked her phone again but didn't see a response from Flint. The self-doubts came pouring in. They hadn't taken pictures like that in a while, and it was stupid of her to send that photo. *He's running for office, for crying out loud. But at least my face wasn't in it, and I turned the lights low.*

She tipped the wineglass to her lips and let the liquid flow down her throat. *What the hell was I thinking?*

The more she thought about it, the more her flight or fight instinct kicked into gear. It wouldn't take her long to get back to her apartment...

Her phone's screen lit up. She stared the phone down, willing it to light up again without her having to touch it. Rae took a deep breath and checked her notifications.

Flint: *I hope you aren't tired tonight. I should be there in 30.*

6

Rae answered the knock on her door with a smirk. "Took you twenty-eight minutes to get here."

"This will take a lot longer than that." Flint stepped forward, leading Rae to step backward. He did it once more and closed the door with a thud. Before he could remove his coat, he stepped forward once again, kissed Rae, and in one swift motion, had her back pressed against the wall. His kiss turned rough as their tongues became intertwined. His hands moved from her face, down the curves of her body. This is what home felt like. He was her home.

Those thoughts quickly left her mind when he broke the kiss, took a small step back, and helped Rae remove the tank top from her body. She stood there looking at him in a daze.

"You know, I wish you would have kept that shirt on you had earlier."

Rae tried to catch her breath as she asked, "Why is that?"

"Because I was hoping to rip it off."

He stalked over and was on her in seconds, his body flush against hers. His hands and lips were everywhere as she felt her brain short-circuiting because her nerves were frayed. His breath on her lips when he took a small break from kissing her made her quiver. She felt their bodies moving backward down the hall, making their way toward the bedroom without breaking contact. About halfway there, he had enough and lifted her up, and she reacted by wrapping her legs around his waist and her fingers through his hair. Within seconds, they made it to his bedroom, and he had unclipped her bra. In a flash, her hands were out of his hair as she slipped the straps down her arms and threw her bra some-where in the room. Rae felt the gears in her mind begin to work again and placed her hands on his chest to halt him. The look on his face mirrored a five-year-old who had been told that they couldn't have cookies before dinner.

"You have way too many clothes on."

She smirked as she undid his tie at a painstakingly slow pace. Rae thought she might have heard him growl, and she let out a low snicker. "Patience is a virtue." She had finally finished undoing his tie and placed her hand on his chest. The pounding of his heart under her hand made her body quiver.

"One that I don't have." If Rae had to guess, it took him about two-point-five seconds to step back from her touch and remove his button-down shirt and slacks. She was sure she heard at least one button hit the floor as it flew off his shirt, but they could take the time to figure that out later.

Seconds later, his hands were all over her once more. His fingers moved quickly, yet thoroughly over her body as if he was examining every inch of her. The moan that left her lips bounced off of the walls in the room.

"You're so beautiful," he said as his head traveled down to

her breasts with light touches and licks. Her moans increased as his mouth and hands set her body ablaze. They threw any thoughts besides finding ecstasy out of the window. He lazily made his way down her body and landed right where she wanted him. His fingers splayed over her thighs before they curved under the sides of her panties and slipped them down over her legs. Flint continued to take his sweet time worshipping her body.

Rae waited in anticipation of what he would do next. "Think you can move faster?"

"Now who isn't being patient?" With that, his lips landed back on hers, silencing any remarks on the tip of her tongue to his comment.

RAE WOKE UP AND GROANED. She opened one eye and gazed out the window and saw that it was dark outside, but the illumination from the street lights cast a soft glow in the room. She searched through the covers, trying to get her bearings and touch Flint, but came up empty on both.

"Flint?" she whispered, in case he was still asleep in bed. No answer.

Rae wiped some sleep from her eyes and turned over and fished for her phone in the covers. Once she found it and saved it from the floor below after it almost slipped out of her hands, Rae saw that it was 1:06 a.m. She was annoyed that she was awake at this time of night but knew that there was nothing she could do about it now. She swept the covers off her body, thankful that she thought to put on her comfortable clothes before she had fallen asleep. There was still a slight chill in the air, but she would have been downright freezing without the clothes or Flint and the blankets keeping her warm. Rae picked up a thick red cardigan and threw it on to replace the warmth she missed from the cocoon she had made in her covers.

Rae stood up and walked around the bed and saw, through a crack in the door, that a light in the living room was on. Putting two and two together, she guessed that Flint must have gone out there because he couldn't sleep, or he was up working on campaign things.

"Hey, why are you up?" Rae said as she came into the living room.

Flint looked up from his laptop and gave her a tired smile. She wasn't shocked to find him in a black short sleeve t-shirt and thin pajama bottoms while she was wondering if they were currently living in the Arctic. "Just finished a wrap-up call with the team."

Maybe that woke her up. She shook her head as she looked at him from her position in the hallway. She wasn't shocked that he had been on a call with his campaign team. There had been many nights where Flint had been up at all hours of the night trying to get things done, and that was beside his day job as a lawyer.

"Is it something that can wait until morning? You need your sleep."

Flint yawned, further proving her point. "I'm just wrapping up a couple of things, and then I'll come to bed. I should be done in five minutes."

"Is this actually five minutes, or is it more like twenty-five?"

Flint snorted, and she knew it was because she had a

point. "I mean actually five minutes. You're right. I'm beat, and I need to get more rest."

"Say that again?"

Flint licked his lips and said, "You're right."

"And don't you forget it. Plus, you need your rest after the exhilarating workout you did only a few hours ago." With that, Rae headed back into the bedroom, laughing to herself.

THE PERSON RAN a hand through their hair. They had been at this for two hours tops, and it was taking way longer than they thought it would.

A quick glance at the clock confirmed that it was 1:06 a.m. A single stretch and a gulp of the remaining coffee in their mug only gave a tiny sense of satisfaction. The person stared into their mug, debating with themselves if it made sense to get more coffee.

Shrugging it off for now, they continued on their mission. They were sure that at some point, their right index finger would fall off given how many times they had left-clicked on their mouse. A few more clicks on an arrow pointed right finally led them to what they had been looking for.

"Bingo."

7

"You know we could just order takeout, right? I can save this for another night," Rae said, gesturing to the food in front of her. "Hell, we can make this tomorrow."

"No, I promised you we would have more frequent date nights, and we made plans to have one tonight."

"But you look dead on your feet." That wasn't a lie. There were bags forming under his eyes. She knew it was a result of him staying up all times of the night to finish the mountain of work he had. It was several days later after Rae had caught him on his computer at one in the morning.

"I'm fine. Let's cook, okay?"

Rae noted the testiness in his tone but didn't comment on it. While she was mincing garlic and he was chopping onions, Flint's phone rang. Both he and Rae glanced at the phone before turning back to their respective jobs.

When Flint's phone rang again, he announced, "I'm not answering it."

"Flint, you know how this will end up. You declare that

you're not responding and then it nags at you because the person keeps trying to contact you. Then I get fed up and tell you to answer the phone. It's a cycle that never ends."

Flint sighed and put the knife down. He turned to Rae and said, "You're right." The ringing stopped.

"I'm afraid that this is—" The ringing started again. Rae closed her eyes and took a deep breath before looking into Flint's eyes. "Our new normal. Flint, someone wants to get in contact with you. Answer the phone." The person on the other end of the line hung up once more.

"Fine." He walked over to the sink and washed his hands. During the time it took him to wash and dry his hands, the phone started ringing again.

"It's Rick. I'll take this in the living room."

"Shocker," Rae said as she went back to mincing garlic.

A few moments went by with Rae being able to hear Flint's voice every now and again, but she kept her mind focused on the tasks at hand.

"Babe."

Rae jumped at the sound of Flint's voice. "Can you make a little noise?" She chuckled as he walked up to her from her left. "Scared the shit out of me."

Whereas Rae's laughter would have usually caused Flint to grin, this time, it had no effect. When she looked at him over her shoulder, his face was stoic. She saw the vein in his neck was pulsating and more prevalent than normal. "What's wrong? Why are you upset?"

"Can we talk? You might want to sit down for this."

Rae followed along as Flint led her to her living room couch. She had chosen shades of blue and white to form a welcoming environment and to calm her down when she was stressed, but the colors did little to add tranquility to her mind.

"Flint, what happened?"

"Someone leaked a photo of you."

Rae stared at him, not comprehending what he said. "Someone leaked a photo of me? What photo?" She knew she sounded silly repeating what he had just said, but that was the only thing she could say.

Flint nodded before he continued. "It's a—" The ringing of Rae's cell phone interrupted Flint. She scanned the room quickly before finding her phone next to the TV on her television stand. "It's Eve."

"You should answer it. I wouldn't be surprised if she is calling about the same thing I was trying to tell you."

Rae answered the phone mid-ring. "Hey, girl."

"Are you sitting? Is Flint there? You might want to sit down for this."

"Okay, it's scary how well you both assumed I would need to sit down for this. What's up? What picture got leaked?"

Flint already had his phone in his hand and scrolled through his apps until he found the one he wanted. He turned his phone over to Rae, and she gasped before her stare turned into a glare.

"You've gotta be kidding me."

On his screen was a photo of Rae taking a body shot off of a man. Although the man was shirtless, someone had placed the shot glass on the guy's stomach, and Rae had been in the process of grabbing the shot with her mouth. She was dressed up in a pink crown and sash that she remembered said, "21st birthday."

"Seriously? Someone took the time to dig this up? I was

celebrating my twenty-first birthday my junior year of college, and it was a dare. Eve, I swore you took the photo, but it's been a while since I've looked at the photo, and that night is a blur. It's an old photo, and I didn't see that guy after that. Who cares?"

"Rick and my other campaign staff do. I do."

Rae turned to Flint and raised an eyebrow at the tone of his voice and the look on his face. She asked, "Why? It's a picture that's over eight years old. I was still in college, and it meant nothing. I was just having fun."

It was then time for Flint's phone to ring again, and Rae couldn't stop herself from rolling her eyes. "Is it Rick?" Flint nodded. "Please turn your ringer off so we can talk about this before he tries to blame this entire thing on me." Flint took a deep breath, and Rae watched as some tension left his face as he did what she asked and turned his phone's ringtone off.

"Rae, back when this photo was taken, this wouldn't have been a big deal. But now, in the age of social media and a changing political climate, this is a big enough deal to get people talking. We need to figure out how someone got this photo. I know I locked down my account when I started my current job, and you changed your security settings right before you and Flint started dating again. I remember because you asked me what settings I changed on my account."

Rae turned toward her phone and noted the seriousness in Eve's voice. "Is this going to affect Flint's odds of winning the congressional seat?"

"Since Flint is well-known because of his job, charity work, and family besides running for office, I would say it might. At the very least, it would raise the profile of this race.

And this photo will be shown all over the internet in a few hours. We were on the shortlist of media outlets that found out a few hours early."

That thought sobered her up even more. She glanced at her phone before looking over at Flint, who hadn't said a word recently. "Can we go after this person? Who the heck would try to leak a photo of me that could easily be explained away?" After a moment of silence in the room, Rae answered her own question, "That doesn't matter. It's being released for shock value."

"There you go."

Rae barely heard Eve's comment before Flint's phone vibrated on the table. Rae glanced at the device before looking back at Flint.

"That's probably Rick."

"I wouldn't bet against you."

"Good."

Flint's eyebrows rose, and his mouth was slightly agape. She assumed he hadn't expected her to say that was good. "We need to figure out how to slow this story down and nail whoever did this."

8

I t didn't take long for Rick to call a meeting of Flint's top campaign staff. Flint offered to have the meeting in his living room, and he and Rae busied themselves with making their guests feel comfortable when they arrived. The couple gathered coffee pods and snacks because they both figured it would be a long night dealing with the potential aftermath of the photo.

"While everyone else is drinking coffee, can I have a glass of wine? I think the examination of this photo will make me even more of a nervous wreck. Emphasis on the even more part," Rae asked Flint as she held up a bottle of her favorite blend, showing it to him from her place in the kitchen.

"To be honest, I don't blame you. But I also don't think the meeting will be that bad."

"That's because a photo of you isn't getting scrutinized."

Flint sighed before looking back over at Rae. "I've been scrutinized before too. Not on this large of a scale, but I understand what it feels like. It's an invasion of privacy, something no one really thinks can happen to them until it does. And when it does, it hurts a lot."

Rae sighed and placed the wine bottle down on the counter. She turned to lean against the counter and rubbed her hands over her eyes. She then leaned back farther, letting her head rest on her shoulders as she tried to get any kinks and tension out of her neck. When she stood straight up, Flint was on his way into the kitchen. He stopped in front of her and brushed away a curl that had landed on her shoulder.

"We'll get through this together. Okay?"

Rae closed her eyes again before nodding. When she opened them again, Flint's face helped ease some anxiety she had been feeling.

"I love you, and we'll figure this out." He pulled Rae into his embrace, and she felt a sense of warmth and peace.

"I love you too."

Someone interrupted their moment when there was a knock on the door.

"I'll be right back."

Rae took a few deep breaths and rocked back and forth on her heels. When she leaned a little too far back and hit the counter, she decided that it was time to face the music. She walked out into the dining room and was greeted by Flint's campaign team. Rick was sitting in the chair closest to Flint, and Kate, the deputy campaign director, was sitting in another chair across from Rick. Next to Kate was Jean, the fundraising director, and next to her was Jill, Flint's spokesperson.

"It's great that all of you could join us on short notice. I know some of the team is also joining us by phone. Thank you, too, for taking the time to join this phone call." Flint gestured to his team in the room and to the telephone.

With that, the meeting began. Suggestions about who could have leaked the image flew around first.

"We need to look at Rob Cohen first and foremost. He would have the most to gain by the leak." Rob was Flint's opponent in the primary race for the open congressional seat. There were many entrants in the race, but both Flint and Rob were polling near the top so far. Rob, an accountant, was making a name for himself by running on messaging about the economy and budget. A scandal could jumble their favorability.

"Excellent point. Is there anyone else we think might be responsible for this?"

"Don't forget, a few months ago, Rae was stalked and threatened. Although my mother was involved, I highly doubt she would have done it, given how this would hurt the campaign. I don't know if I can say the same about her friends who were also involved in the scheme."

"That's right. It also came up when we researched both of you based on the answers you gave us and our own preliminary research."

Rae narrowed her eyes at Rick. Although she assumed they had done research on her, she didn't appreciate being told how extensive it was in a room full of people. She shifted her eyes over to Flint and made a mental note to ask him about that later.

The meeting continued, and after several minutes most of the group came to a consensus: they would release a statement condemning the leaking of the photo, and they would hire a consultant to make sure they increased the security on all of their social media and technological devices. As the group was gathering their things, Rick's voice stopped them.

"There's one more thing. Rae, it might be helpful if you cleaned up your image a bit."

Rae did a double-take because she couldn't believe the words that had flown out of his mouth.

"What do you mean, clean up my image? I do nothing now." Rae's glare wasn't leaving her face anytime soon. "Why should I adjust the way I do things when I've done nothing wrong? I'm the victim here!" She felt Flint lay his hand on her lower back, but it did little to relieve the anger she was feeling.

"I understand completely. It was just a suggestion to maybe dress up more in your everyday life. For example, when you go to happy hour or to any exercise classes. Still go out to happy hour with your friends, but don't drink as much. Things like that."

"That is creepy because I didn't give you permission to dig into my life that much."

Flint stepped in between Rae and Rick and said, "Rick. I've warned you several times I didn't want this campaign to affect Rae's day-to-day life. We had an agreement that we would try to prevent this from taking over."

"Yes, I know. But that was before a photo of her taking a body shot off someone leaked to the media. You both need to be on your A-game now. The world is watching."

Days later, Rae was still pissed over Rick's words. She needed to change, to act more proper. What she wanted to do was to lie low until this all blew over. But she still needed to work, do every day errands, and to live her own life.

They released the photo several hours after the meeting with Flint's team. In the age of social media, the photo took the internet by storm but didn't become as big of a catastrophe as the campaign thought. Rae was fortunate to have enough time to warn her job that a photo of her from several years ago was being released without her consent, and they offered to support her 110%.

"When we find out who did this, I'd be happy to knock them on their ass. Incognito and stealth-like, though, because I don't want this getting tied back to you guys."

Rae snorted. "Thanks, Liv, I truly appreciate it."

"You know what she means, though. We have your back."

Rae smiled for the first time in days. Although she wanted to be alone, she was happy that Eve, Liv, and Jules had called her to find out how she was doing. Her family and friends had rallied behind to support her too, but she couldn't shake Rick's words from her mind. Was changing parts of herself to fit into this image they wanted to portray really the answer?

She'd taken a week off of work to be alone and to hang out with Flint when he was available. Although it felt like the world was crashing around her, being able to stay in her own little bubble was nice.

The one pleasurable thing about being in the social media age is that the leaking of her photo became old news quickly. Well, that was because of the cease and desist letters that were fired off at every opportunity.

Although the news had died, and as far as she could see she wasn't being followed, she had had little relief. Her phone's text notifications brought her out of the self-imposed misery.

Eve: Rae, you're coming to happy hour, right? We haven't seen you in a long time.

Rae: I don't know, ladies. I'm already in yoga pants and sitting on my couch. You know what time it is when that happens.

Liv: It usually means you're in for the night, but you could come and hang out with us.

Rae: I dunno, I'm mentally exhausted.

Jules: Understandable, given what happened. But try to get out every once in a while.

Liv: And going to the mailbox to check your mail doesn't count.

Rae chuckled at Liv's text. She looked at her phone and noticed that if she started moving now, she would only be about a half-hour late to the happy hour. And it wasn't like she was usually between ten to twenty minutes late to them regularly anyway.

Rae: Okay, you got me. Going to take a shower now.

9

"Looks like I should set up that camera again." Rae pulled at her navy blue sweater before reaching up to tighten her high ponytail. In her opinion, her sweater, jeans, and flats made a cute ensemble that wouldn't cause a fuss with the campaign. They could deal with the ponytail.

She thought about how Flint had helped her set up a camera to watch the outside of her apartment back when she was getting threatening messages. She rubbed her temples as she tried to process the fact that someone was trying to come after her again.

"That wouldn't be a terrible idea. Or maybe you could move in with Flint. Didn't you mention that he had a nice apartment with security and all of that?"

Rae didn't understand how she didn't have whiplash, given how fast she turned her head to glare at Liv. Liv's lips were twitching, trying to fight to keep a straight face.

"His apartment is fantastic and in a wonderful part of

town. But there's one major problem even if I was to consider this: Flint hasn't asked me to move in with him."

"Yeah…it would be kind of awkward just showing up at his apartment, suitcases in hand."

Rae nodded. "Yep." She paused with an eyebrow raised. "Only kind of awkward…"

"Have you and Flint talked about moving in together?"

It looked like she'd lost Jules based on the expression on her face. "We talked about it briefly a few months ago, but with the campaign ramping up, we haven't found the time to discuss it anymore."

"There's always time to discuss things that are important. You just have to make an effort." And now it was three against one with Eve bringing up the rear.

Rae sighed, "I know. I don't want to be the one that brings it up. I don't know how he feels about it."

"Do you have things over at his house? Does he have things at yours?"

Rae thought about Liv's questions for a second before responding. "We do."

"And how much time do you spend at your apartment by yourself?"

"I was going to say I'm there all the time because of Flint's schedule, but to be honest, Flint is always coming over to my apartment, or I'm heading over to his since we hardly see—" Rae stopped mid-thought and tossed her ponytail over her shoulder. None of the other women said anything, but she could hear their thoughts anyway. It was silly at this point to not at least talk to Flint about moving in together. It would be taking a bigger step in their relationship, but at what cost? Especially with all the craziness surrounding his run for Congress. Would he even want to make another big life change at the moment? "I'll think about it."

The other ladies seemed happy with that response.

"We did briefly start talking about our dreams and goals outside of what's going on with the campaign."

"Oh, really? That's awesome and a great next step in the relationship. It's important to see if your ideals match up for a potential future together." Rae could see that Eve couldn't stop the corners of her lips from rising and turning into a smirk.

"That's what I was thinking too. And I think it's great that he isn't trying to hide me, you know?"

Liv coughed on her drink. "Why would he try to hide you?"

"You'd be surprised what some campaigns do in order to win. I guess I'm less fortunate in that they only asked me to clean up my image. Which is hilarious because I practically do nothing now?"

"We had some wild times in college, though."

Eve's words made Rae laugh before she could hide it. "You aren't lying about that." Rae held up her drink and clinked it together with Eve's before they took another sip.

"You know." Rae removed her eyes from her glass and peered at Eve. "This might be the perfect opportunity to start working on that article about you and Flint. Did you hear anything back from Flint?"

"He seemed open to it, but I assume he wants to get input from his team, so I'll let you know when I hear something else about it. I think you're right, though. Starting to put something together now would probably be helpful. Let me ask again. With everything going on, it might have slipped his mind."

"Understandable."

Rae leaned back in her chair. "I still can't wrap my head around why someone would want to leak the photos, though. Especially one that could easily be proven to be years old."

"Just because a photo is old, doesn't mean it isn't valuable to the right person. I've been thinking about this a lot because let's be real. It's the only thing I've been able to think about right now."

Eve shook her finger before she gestured to Rae and said, "Rae, you might be onto something. It sounds like this person is...desperate? I'm not sure how else to describe it."

"What do you mean?" asked Liv. She placed her phone down and turned toward Eve.

"Hunting down a photo of someone from their twenty-first birthday that took place a long time ago is ridiculous. It's like they didn't have access to any other photos."

"Or maybe it's a test run."

Rae flipped her head around to look at Liv. "What do you mean a test run?"

Liv placed her hand on Rae's briefly before bringing it up to her chin. "This isn't me trying to freak you out or anything. But like Eve said, a photo from college is a silly thing to bring up from the grave. I have buried plenty of things that took place in college, and I could only hope that they stay that way." She visibly shuttered before continuing. "The only way, at least to me, it makes sense to bring a photo from college up is if it is something despicable. As far as my millennial mind can see, this photo is just some fun being had by several people. And as we all now can see, this made a slight dent in the media before everyone's attention was diverted to other things. I'm sure Eve can back me up on this."

Eve nodded her head. "We covered the initial leak, but we've moved on. Which is great news for you."

"And the campaign," Rae added before turning to Liv. "So, you're suggesting that this person might be holding on to their big weapon. Figuratively, not literally."

All Liv did was nod before grabbing a beer. With that, Rae stood up.

"Where are you going?" Jules asked as she looked up at Rae just before she started walking away.

"To get some whiskey. This wine won't cut it, and I couldn't care less if Rick is keeping tabs on me."

FOR THE REST of the night, Rae nursed the whiskey that she ordered, figuring that having only one would not lead to anyone taking her photo or writing up a story that would end up in Rick's inbox that night. Hanging out with her friends gave her some relief from the tension that had been building over the last few days.

But as she lay in bed that night, Rick's words were still at the forefront of her brain.

Before she could turn out her lamp for the night, there was a knock on her door. Checking her phone to make sure she wasn't missing anything, she grabbed it before she headed toward her door. *Did I ever unpack that baseball bat I bought a while back?*

As she walked past her living room, she grabbed the hoodie she had haphazardly thrown over the back of her couch and put it on. *Who the heck would knock at my door at this time of night?* As if they had heard her inner thoughts, the person knocked on her door once more. She peeped through the peephole and saw that it was Flint standing on her doorstep. With a sigh of relief, she opened the door and stared.

"Why didn't you call to say you were coming over? I almost panicked because someone was knocking on my door at 11:15 p.m. Is everything okay?"

"Yeah, everything is okay. I just had to see you."

"Are you sure everything is okay? I thought we were planning on seeing each other tomorrow evening. This isn't me attempting to throw you out."

Flint grinned before he said, "For the better part of the past couple of months, we've slept in the same bed together, and then tonight we didn't. I couldn't stand it, so I came over to fix the problem. I missed you, Rae."

"I missed you too. Even if you scared the shit out of me."

"Sorry about that. I'm so tired I can barely keep my eyes open."

"Okay. Why don't you head to my bedroom and get ready for bed, and I'll make sure everything is locked up here?"

All Flint did was nod and walk away. Rae went to the lock on her front door and double-checked that everything was locked. She remembered that she had left some dishes in the sink and finished those up before she headed back to her bedroom. What greeted her made her chuckle to herself.

Flint had gotten into bed and was sitting up with his back against the headboard. But he had fallen asleep. His head was slumped over with his chin on his chest, eyes closed, and breathing even and deep. She climbed into bed on the other side of him and took his phone out of his hand. Rae then tapped him to wake him up so he could get into a more comfortable position before turning off the lamp on her side of the bed. He groaned a bit but didn't wake up as he molded himself to fit her body. She soon fell asleep in his arms, their warmth wrapping around her like a cocoon.

10

"How's everything going? I'm sorry your father couldn't be here. You know his job always has him on the go." Rae's father, Jake Carter, traveled extensively for an enormous tech company in the area.

"It just means that I have to see you guys more often. That's a loaded question, Mom." Rae took a sip of the wine that their waiter had placed in front of her moments ago. "The picture leaking, even though it was from years ago, could still damage my reputation and my job. We're fine, or as fine as I assume a significant other is when their partner is busy all the time."

Stella Carter eyed her daughter before replying. "Have you been able to prove that Eve took the photo while you both were in college?"

Rae nodded before taking the time to look around the restaurant. It had a peaceful ambiance that gave Rae a sense of ease, even though they were talking about a tense subject.

"Yeah. We can trace back to when the photo was taken since Eve still had the original file. It's helpful that Eve posted them on social media since that contains dates. Plus, who didn't get drunk in college and take silly photos? It's like a rite of passage."

"Did Flint or his campaign say anything?"

"I think Flint was shocked at first but has been super supportive. The campaign is a bit worried, though. They've come up with ways that I can brush this under the rug." That was an understatement.

"Oh, yeah?" Stella took a sip of her water before looking her daughter in the eye.

Rae hesitated before replying, "They said I could change up my appearance, do a few more events, and that might change how people perceive me."

Rae watched her mother digest the news and could read every emotion on her face. She went from being worried to shocked to angry in a matter of seconds.

"You're perfect the way you are. You don't need to change yourself for anyone. I've always taught you that."

"I know, Mom."

"Plus, those photos are eight years old. From when you were in college. Why should that be hanging over your head now?"

All Rae could do was shrug. "Apparently, it matters in this arena. The last thing I want to do is hurt Flint's chances at winning this race—"

"Rae, I didn't expect to see you here."

Rae whipped around to find the person who was talking to her. "Sarah? I haven't seen you in forever. I didn't know you moved back to D.C."

"Yep. Still down here. Sorry to interrupt your lunch

with... your mother? Hi, I'm not sure if you remember me. I'm Sarah, Rae's old roommate."

Rae could see that her mother was trying to place her, so she gave her a little guidance. "Back when I lived in D.C. When I first dated Flint."

"Sarah! Oh, hi, dear. It's lovely to see you again. How have you been?" Rae wasn't sure if her mother remembered Sarah or was trying to be nice. It didn't matter in the grand scheme of things.

"I'm doing well. Well, I don't want to interrupt your lunch any longer, but Rae, we should get together sometime and catch up. Maybe grab a coffee or go to a happy hour."

It took everything in Rae to not question Sarah's sudden interest in her, but she shrugged those feelings off. "Sure, whenever works best for you. My phone number is still the same."

Sarah nodded and said, "Sounds good, I'll be in touch. It was lovely seeing you both again!" With that, Sarah went on her way and headed out of the restaurant.

Rae asked the question that had been on the tip of her tongue since Sarah interrupted them. "Mom, did you remember Sarah, or was that all an act?"

"I vaguely remembered her. Couldn't pinpoint her in a crowd, but remembered that she was hardly around when I came to visit you or helped you move in."

"Yeah, that's the thing. She was hardly there when I was home, and I even offered to have her join me and the girls at happy hour. So, I'm shocked she wants to hang out with me."

"Maybe she regrets not hanging out with you more?"

Rae laughed. "Could be. I'm sure there are a million people who feel the same way."

"You never know. After all, you touched Flint's life, and he was willing to do whatever it took to get you back in his."

"Mom, my company hired him to do some work for the nonprofit that I work for through the firm he works for. Nothing more, nothing less."

Stella raised an eyebrow at her daughter. "Well, didn't he talk to Jules about you before then? When he got back into town?"

Rae thought about her mother's response and nodded her head. "That's true."

"I think you should talk to Flint about why he works with Wild Parks, Wild Lands. And stop believing in big coincidences."

Rae stared at her mother like she didn't know her. "Mom, why don't you just tell me what's up?"

Stella's eyes looked everywhere but at her daughter before she finally took a deep breath. Her eyes migrated up to her daughter's once again, and she said, "Flint talked to me before you guys got back together. Well, *talk* is a powerful word. Emailed me is better."

Rae placed both hands down on the table in front of her and leaned forward. "Flint did what?"

Stella nodded and looked down at her hands. "It was nothing. I didn't fill him in on much, just to let him know you were okay, but he mentioned that he would talk to Jules after I confirmed that you two were still friends."

"So, Flint did his homework."

"I think that's a good assumption."

"Not that any of this matters, but I'll talk to him about it. I'm shocked he talked to you after everything that went on when we broke up. He had to have searched for your email address and all that because I don't think you ever emailed each other before."

Stella nodded. "My whole point in telling you this is that you've touched many people's lives. You shouldn't change who you are just to fit in a box that someone wants to put you in. But yes, definitely talk to Flint about it. Now, tell me more about Sarah."

Before Rae could respond, their waiter returned and asked if they wanted anything else. The two debated what food they wanted to eat before placing an order. Stella took one piece of bread that their waiter left for them and dipped it into some olive oil before setting it on the small plate in front of her. "Back to Sarah."

"What's up with the focus on her?"

"You know I don't believe in coincidences. So, Sarah..."

Rae shook her head at her mother before continuing, "There isn't a lot to say about Sarah. I have no hard feelings against her. We were roommates when I was getting my feet wet in D.C. Honestly, I hardly saw her because she had a steady boyfriend and hung out at his apartment all the time. On the rare occasion that we saw each other, she was nice. But we didn't really do any cool bonding type of activities or things like that. Maybe movie night every so often, but that was it. Last I heard, she moved back home to Milwaukee just as I moved out on my own into a studio apartment. Was never late with her portion of the rent or bills. We were boring in terms of roommate drama."

"At least that's good. Well, I guess you'll see what's up when she contacts you. How's work going?"

"It's going. We're trying to get our legislative goals passed before things really get busy, especially since this is an election year." Rae could see in her mother's eyes that Stella wanted her to elaborate, but Rae just shrugged. "It's fine, Mom."

The look on Stella's face told Rae that she didn't believe that lie, but she dropped the questioning. The two women continued to enjoy their meals and chatted about random things like celebrity gossip.

The duo finished their meal, paid, and Rae took her mother back to her childhood home. Once Rae had the car in park in the driveway, Stella turned to her only child and said, "I know you're working a lot and trying to balance these things. I didn't understand how swamped your life is at the moment. If you need anything, please let me know."

Rae shook her head and pinched the bridge of her nose. It was the only thing that was holding the tears that threatened to fall from her eyes. "Thanks. I wasn't exactly forthcoming with information about everything." She sighed before she continued. "It's been a lot. Between having to deal with Flint's race and the fallout from that photo, my job, and trying to find time for my relationship, my friends, and family... It's been hectic trying to balance it all."

"It's okay to not be okay, sweetheart."

Those words unleashed the floodgates. Rae couldn't keep it together anymore and quietly sobbed into her hands. She felt her mother's arms reach across her car's center console and pull her into an embrace. Although it was a bit of an awkward angle, Rae welcomed her mom's comfort.

"Baby, you're dealing with a lot, but I promise that there is a light at the end of the tunnel."

All Rae could do was nod her head. The tears kept coming, no matter how much Rae tried to stop them. She moved her hands and placed her head on her mother's shoulder. Stella murmured soft, comforting words to her only child while she softly ran her hands through Rae's hair.

When Rae could finally gain control of her emotions, she removed herself from her mother's hug and sat back in her seat. She tried to wipe her eyes and remove the evidence of her crying from her face, and when she opened her eyes, her mother was holding a tissue in her hand, ready for Rae to grab.

"I used to tease your grandmother about her having so many tissues in her purse...now look at me."

Rae smiled because her mother's comment brought up fond memories of her departed grandmother. "Yeah, doesn't Dad say that you're becoming more and more like her every day?"

Stella rolled her eyes and smiled. "Your father says a lot of things." She cleared her throat and said, "Are you feeling any better? Come on inside, and we can continue our mother-daughter day with some wine and a good movie or show?"

Although Rae had some things to do, she couldn't think of anything that she needed to do right this second. "That sounds good. Could you hand me my purse? I'll let Flint know that we're hanging out for a while longer and that I'll see him later."

Stella handed Rae her purse, and she took it and her phone out of the center console. Once the two were inside the Carter home, Rae fired off a text to Flint, letting him know where she was. Not expecting a response, she put her phone back in her bag and sat down on the couch as her mother entered the room with two wine glasses. She handed Rae one glass and then placed hers on the coffee table as she grabbed the remote and tried to find something on television for them to watch.

"So, how are things with Flint?"

"What do you mean? I talked about how busy our lives are, and now I have some questions after what you told me earlier."

"Yes, but that's not talking about how you two are doing personally."

Rae knew what her mother was getting at with her initial question, but she wasn't sure how to answer it. "I think we're fine. It's just been hard to find a decent balance between work and our relationship, but we're trying."

"That's good. And how are the girls?"

"They're good. We should all be getting together soon to hang out. Maybe I'll even host another sleepover because it feels like we haven't seen each other outside of attending something for Flint's campaign or seeing each other one-on-one versus as a group."

"Sounds great." Stella finally settled on a show and turned to her daughter. "Is this okay?"

Rae looked up at the show and smiled. Her mother would have found reruns of *Law and Order Special Victims Unit*, one of her favorite crime dramas that always seemed to be on no matter the time or day. "You know I'm always down to watch this." She grabbed her phone out of her bag to check it once more but saw no messages. She placed her phone back on the coffee table and settled in to watch television with her mom.

Several hours later, Rae felt a sense of relief. Hanging out with her mother had recharged her mental batteries, and she felt like she could take on the world. She stood up and stretched and gave her mom an enormous hug before saying their goodbyes. Once Rae was out the door, she checked her phone and saw that she had several messages from her friends, but nothing from Flint. Although that bothered her, she tried not to let it get to her too much because she needed to focus on the one hundred million other things that she needed to do. Before she pulled out of her parents' driveway, she sent a message to her friends.

Rae: Hey, do you guys want to have a sleepover and head to barre class the next morning? We can work it around all of our schedules, although that might be difficult.

Just as Rae was about to put her phone down to get ready to drive, the device buzzed.

Liv: I'm there if wine is included.

Rae shook her head. She threw her phone down in the passenger's seat and pulled out of her parents' driveway. She shifted into drive and started the trip back to her apartment.

She didn't notice the car idling a few houses away that also pulled out of its parking space and followed her down the street.

11

About a week later, Rae sidestepped someone as they came whizzing by her with a box in their hands. If she had been a second too slow, that person would have crashed into her. She didn't let that near accident deter her from reaching her destination.

Rae was on her way to a volunteer event for Flint's campaign. She could tell that several people were watching her as she maneuvered her way through the crowds to get to the table that bore Flint's name. When someone almost crashed into her again, she was thankful that she could wear sneakers to this event, making it easy for her to dodge and weave out of the way.

"Hey, Rick. Where do you want me?" Rae said as she reached the table. Rick glanced up and gave a small wave. She would count his reaction as a win.

"Glad you didn't have any trouble finding us. Flint's over there talking to some potential constituents. You can head over there or help Kate at the other table."

Rae weighed the two options and figured it was best to let

Flint get to know the people he would represent if he won on his own. She gave her outfit a quick once-over, and before she took a step, Rick said her name.

"The profile that Eve Jackson wants to do sounds like a good idea. I'm sure both Flint and Eve will have more details to share with you, but I wanted to let you know that everything was a go as of a few minutes ago."

"Sounds good." Rae wondered if a meteorite was about to hit Earth because Rick was being nice to her. It took every ounce of control not to look around to see if someone was recording her to catch her reaction to his pleasantries.

Before she thought about causing a scene, she headed over to the main campaign table. The table had a huge sign stating Vote for Flint West hanging off the front of it and red and blue balloons attached to weights to prevent the balloons from flying away. She saw some more balloons off in a corner and deduced that those were probably for giving out to little children whose parents walked up to the table. On the table were flyers announcing Flint's positions on issues important to the district along with several swag items, including pens and buttons. The table was under a tent to protect staffers and constituents from the elements if necessary.

When she finished checking out the table, she approached Kate, who turned around and greeted her. "Thank goodness you're here. I need some help with handing out stickers and balloons. Is that okay?"

She took a deep breath and nodded her head. Talking to congressional members in a meeting was one thing. Having friends around as a safety net to help when talking to strangers was another. Meeting total strangers that might have seen her taking body shots off of someone else? That was a whole different ball game. *I can do this. I know I can.*

The small pep talk she gave herself was all she had to go on when she smiled toward a couple that was coming toward her. She handed them a sticker and asked them to vote for Flint in the upcoming primary. Rae got into a rhythm, and before she knew it, people were actually waiting to talk to her.

One mother walked over with a child, and Rae smiled and greeted her. She then bent down to talk to her daughter, who couldn't have been over five.

"What's your name?"

"Jill."

"Hey, my name is Rae. It's nice to meet you." Rae held out her hand to shake. The child stared at her hand for a few seconds before shaking it.

"Isn't Ray a boy's name?"

Rae smiled before she said, "Not the way I spell it. In fact, my boyfriend over there thought my name was a boy's name when we first met too." She glanced over to look at Flint and was surprised to find him looking back at her. He beamed a smile at her, and she reciprocated before turning her attention back to Jill.

"Would you like a sticker or a balloon? Or both?"

"Both, please!" Rae stood up and reached behind her to grab a sticker off of the table and asked one of the volunteers if she could have a balloon. When she handed both items over to Jill, the little girl grinned, showcasing all of her teeth and the gap in the front where one tooth was missing.

"Jill, we have to leave now. Say goodbye."

"Goodbye, Rae."

Rae waved as the mother and daughter duo left.

As Rae was turning to grab more stickers, she heard a voice behind her.

"You know, I don't think I've ever seen you interact with children."

Rae swung around and looked into the blue eyes that made her feel like she was always at home no matter where they were.

"No one we know really has kids that we interact with regularly."

"That's true. I just found it interesting."

"Noted."

"Hey."

Rae shook her head and smiled at Flint's greeting. "Hey, yourself. Finally catching a break?"

"Yeah, I came over here to grab some water out of the cooler." He gestured to the cooler that Rae was standing in front of.

"Oh, I'm sorry," Rae said as she shifted to the side to allow him to grab a bottle of water. "I guess I could have just reached in there and grabbed it for you."

Flint chuckled. "Don't worry about it." He bent down and grabbed the water before standing back up. Rae was proud of herself for not staring too hard. "Before I came over here, my mom texted me and said that she, Allie, and Lily will be able to come to this event after all, and they should be here shortly."

"Sounds good." Rae had had little interaction with his mother since the colossal blowup over her trying to sabotage their relationship months ago. Rae was happy to at least have Allie and Lily to talk to, although Kate was fun to hang out with when she wasn't busy putting out small fires with Rick.

"I will head back over so I can talk to more people. I'll see you soon." With that, Flint gave her a quick kiss at her temple before heading back over to talk to some people that Rick was entertaining. Rae pulled her attention away from Flint and turned her attention back on talking to more people to get out the word about voting in the primary for Flint West.

She didn't know how much time had passed, but she heard Gladys West before she saw her. Rae took the time to gather her thoughts before she faced Gladys. She figured she wouldn't cause a scene out in public, so Rae was just worried about the awkwardness that would happen as a result of being in the same vicinity.

Rae saw the trio reach the group that had formed around Flint and Rick out of the corner of her eye. She busied herself with straightening up some items on the table while she waited for Rick to direct them to where she was.

"Hey, Rae." Rae held her breath as she turned around and found both of Flint's identical twin sisters behind her.

"Hey! How is everything going? How is New York City?" The twins went to NYU for college and stayed in New York after graduating.

"Everything is going well. Just came down for the weekend to help and see what life is like on the campaign trail," said Allie. Rae thanked her lucky stars that although they were identical, Lily loved dying her hair various colors while Allie kept her hair their natural shade. Made things so much easier when trying to tell them apart.

"Well, we're glad you both could make it. We could always use another set of hands...or two." Rae mentally chastised herself at the corny joke but was relieved to see a smirk appear on Lily's lips. Crisis adverted.

Someone cleared their throat, interrupting the pleasant nature of the moment.

The three women turned their attention to the intrusion.

"Do you mind if I speak to Rae alone?"

Allie and Lily nodded their heads before walking back to the table that Flint's campaign staffers put together.

"Rae, do you mind walking over here? I didn't want anyone to overhear our discussion."

"Sure. That's not a problem." Rae looked over her shoulder as Gladys led the way and saw that Flint was looking at her and not engaging with the conversation he should have been having. His eyebrow shot up, and Rae shrugged before turning around to follow Gladys to a quieter area not too far away. Gladys looked around briefly before focusing on Rae.

"Rae, let me start off by saying I'm sorry."

Rae said nothing in return as she let Gladys's statement hang in the air. She glanced down at her shoes as she wondered where Gladys was going with this. Gladys continued. "We got so caught up in Flint's potential political ambitions that it clouded our judgment." That statement caused Rae to whip her head in Gladys's direction and glare.

"No, in your eyes, I just wasn't good enough for your son."

Gladys stared back at Rae without saying a word. Gladys's cheeks became more inflamed.

"Admit it."

Gladys glanced to her left before sighing and turning her eyes back to Rae. "Yes."

Rae was taken aback by her answer. She hadn't expected her to admit it.

"So, where does that leave us now, Gladys?"

Gladys took a deep breath and said, "My son loves you. That much is clear behind everything that he does. Including the confrontation at the law firm. I don't think I've ever seen him that angry."

Rae nodded her head in agreement. Although they had been out of each other's lives for several years, she knew that she had never seen Flint that angry either.

"None of this had anything to do with you. You and Flint are well matched. I even saw it in the photos that the private investigator took when you first met. Those photos plus his report painted a picture of something I didn't want to admit because we had already had a firm plan in place of how we wanted Flint and Cassandra to be a couple."

"Without Flint's permission? I don't know how much Cassandra knew about this entire scheme."

"She wasn't completely in the dark, but it wasn't hard for Calvin to convince her she was doing the right thing for her family. Didn't hurt that she has also had a crush on Flint for years."

Rae side-eyed Gladys. "That's a lot to put on someone."

"I know, and we shouldn't have done it." Gladys sighed before she continued. "Anyway, I just wanted to apologize again."

Rae nodded her head but didn't have a response for Gladys.

She looked over at Flint for a moment before turning her attention back to Rae. "He has a lot of pressure on him, and I see the calming effect that you have on him. I should have taken the time to get to know you." Gladys paused again. "I'd like to have that opportunity now if you are okay with that."

Rae looked over at Flint, briefly. Without turning her eyes back to Gladys, she said, "To be honest, I can't give you an answer right now. I promise to be respectful, but I still haven't forgiven you for the hell you put us through. That being said, we have one big thing in common." She turned back to Gladys. "We both want to see Flint win that congressional seat, so I'll do what it takes to make it happen."

Gladys stared into Rae's eyes, and Rae watched as she changed before her. Gone was the woman asking for a truce and forgiveness, and in its place was a woman ready to handle business. "You're right. That is of the utmost importance."

Rae stuck her hand out and waited for Gladys to shake it. "To getting Flint into Congress?"

Gladys gave Rae a firm handshake. "To getting Flint into Congress."

As THE MORNING turned to afternoon, the smile on Rae's face grew wearier. Not that she wasn't happy to be there, but after smiling all day, her face was tired. As things were wrapping up for their booth, Rae went to grab a water bottle. As she was about to bend over and open the cooler, a bottle of water appeared in front of her face. She looked to her left and saw Flint holding the bottle with an understanding smile.

"I was walking toward you with this, but you didn't see me."

"Nope. I was determined to make it over here as fast as

possible." She grabbed the bottle from his hand and thanked him. She downed a third of the bottle before she came up for air. "And that's why I was on a mission to get over here. Thanks again for this."

"You're welcome. Everything else go well today?"

"Pretty much. I talked to your mother."

"I saw that. I would have come over and run interference, but I got pulled into a conversation with Rick and some other people."

Rae waved her hand and said, "It was fine. Your mother and I have a common goal and are working toward that goal."

"What are—" Flint's question was cut off when Rick came over to the couple.

"Sorry to interrupt. Flint, I have a reporter here who was hoping to get a couple of quotes from you about today's event. Do you have a minute?" Flint nodded, and Rick waved the reporter over. Rae watched as Flint's entire demeanor changed, transforming between laid-back Flint and professional Flint. He stood up straighter, his face became more serious, and the words that flowed from his lips held even more charm as the reporter recorded Flint's comments. The reporter then asked a question that made Rae's eyes widen.

"How have you both been handling the personal photograph leak?"

The only body part of Rae's that moved was her eyes as she watched Flint out of the corner of her eye. His face could have been made of stone based on how still he was, but his expression gave nothing away. She then glanced at Rick to see his mouth was slightly agape. He wasn't expecting that question either.

When she looked back at Flint, he cleared his throat and

said, "I won't speak for Rae because she can speak for herself. Personally, I hated seeing my girlfriend go through the emotional turmoil that this scandal has brought our way." He made the quote gesture with his hands when he said "scandal." "She didn't ask for her life to be put under a microscope. The amount of integrity and grace that Rae has shown during this time has been phenomenal and has made me fall in love with her even more. I hope this person is found, and justice is served."

Rae's already tired cheeks felt as if they were on fire. She felt herself getting teary-eyed at Flint's words but tried to keep it together. She then looked back at the reporter. "I think Flint said just about everything I wanted to say. The leak of the photos crossed so many boundaries and was an act of betrayal. I hope that whoever did it is ashamed and comes forward." Rae became more choked up as she talked. But she still kept it together. She hoped those words would lead to the person or people who caused all of this mayhem to stop.

Little did she know, these quotes would increase their rage.

12

———

"There are many people at this meet-the-candidates event, huh?" Rae looked around and examined the crowd. Most of her experience with congressional candidates had been at fundraisers or meeting with them and their staff in their offices, not attending a town hall event. Rae was thankful that so many people ended up coming because the weather in the D.C. area had been disarray, going from nice and warmer than normal to a cold front sweeping through in the next several days with threats of snow. March was proving to be a wild month.

"Yeah. I wasn't expecting this, to be honest, but I'm glad people are getting more involved in the political process." Before Flint could say any more, Rick rushed up to him, needing to finalize some last-minute details before Flint took the stage.

Rae felt some nervous energy bouncing off of Flint and did her best to soothe him by squeezing the hand that was holding hers. After she finished surveying the room, she turned her attention back to Flint, who she had caught glancing at her. She hoped he was listening to the things Rick was telling him. Rick walked away a moment later, telling Flint he had about ten minutes before he hit the stage.

"I'll go and take a few moments to prepare and chat with Rick some more. I'll see you on the other side of this thing, okay?"

Rae nodded her head before she gave him a smile. "Good luck. I'll be right here rooting you on from the crowd."

Flint returned the smile and gave her a hug before heading off into the direction that Rick went. Rae went to her seat and snapped her fingers. She forgot to ask if his mom and dad were still coming. Although hanging out with Gladys wasn't the top item on her list of things she wanted to do, she knew she could deal with having to sit next to her for several hours. Plus, with them squaring things away at the county event a couple of weeks ago, she felt more at ease with being in her presence.

"Oh, excuse me."

Rae had spoken them into existence because Terry and Gladys West were standing a few feet away from her. She took a deep breath and stood up to greet Flint's parents.

Terry smiled and gave her a warm handshake before he asked how she was. When she turned to face Gladys, she wasn't sure what to do. Her decision was made for her when Gladys greeted her politely. Awkward crisis adverted.

"Uh, well, I saved you both some seats right here." She gestured to the seats to her left. "I think Rick and another staffer will sit in the two seats over there."

"Thanks for saving seats for us." Terry's voice cracked a bit, but he cleared his throat and continued. "Excuse me.

We're sorry for being late. Gladys just had to grab something before we left."

Gladys walked over to the seat closest to the one Rae had selected for herself and sat down.

"I needed to grab my grandmother's brooch. I wanted to bring it with me, so hopefully, it will bring Flint some good luck."

Terry, who had now sat down in the seat next to his wife, said, "She's convinced it's a lucky charm."

"I wore it the night I met you." The two shared a moment that forced a soft smile onto Rae's lips. The admiration that the couple had for one another was overflowing, and anyone nearby would notice it.

Rick interrupted the threesome when he mentioned that the town hall would start soon. Everyone grabbed their seats and waited for the event to begin.

"AND THAT IS why I'm running to be your representative in Congress."

The crowd went wild at Flint's closing statement. Rae was biased, but she thought Flint had done a phenomenal job dictating his points and getting his message across about how hard he wanted to work for the people of this district. Throughout the time that Flint was up there, she had noticed that one candidate, in particular, kept instigating discussion with Flint. Rae had done some quick research on the candidates running against Flint, and Rob Cohen was at the top of her list. Even though she wasn't a campaign manager or analyst, if she was a betting woman, she would guess that

Rob's campaign had pegged Flint to be the frontrunner based on their attempt to trip him up at any opportunity that he had.

"So, what did you think of that?"

Rae turned around and found herself face-to-face with Gladys. She bit back a sigh and replied, "I thought Flint did really well, but Rob was just a step below bulldog in his attempts to trip him up."

Gladys glanced off to her right before nodding. "I agree. I'm glad I'm not the only one who sensed that."

"Do you know anything about Rob?"

Rae watched as Gladys's gaze moved back to the stage. "He's local too. Sat on the school board for several years. He ran for mayor several years ago and lost. He has a lot of experience running in elections. If I had to guess, he's probably Flint's biggest competitor at the moment."

All the things Gladys had mentioned, Rae had already known, which relieved her and troubled her. She was happy that her research into Rob had dug up some of his history, but she wished Gladys had told her more.

Rae glanced toward the stage, and all thoughts of Rob left her mind. Flint appeared in her line of sight, and her smile was bursting at the seams. He was walking toward them with Rick, who had rushed off to meet him backstage once the event concluded. It took everything in her to not run over to him and give him a hug.

Rae saw Gladys shift slightly out of the corner of her eye, and when she turned to look at her, she caught Gladys looking at her son. Gladys's gaze didn't waver, and when Flint finally looked up, she saw him look at her, then his mom, then back at her. There, his stare remained until he reached the two most important women in his life.

"Rick, thanks for everything tonight. I think the campaign is definitely moving in the right direction." Flint took his eyes off of Rae briefly to look at Rick as he spoke.

"Perfect. I'll send you an email this evening about our next steps, and then we'll chat in the morning." Rick said goodbye to the group before he headed out.

"Mom, thanks for coming," Flint said as he shifted his attention to his mother. Although he wasn't looking at her, Rae's body was aware of Flint's presence. More than she would care to admit.

"Wouldn't miss it for the world, sweetie. You did an outstanding job." She leaned in to give him a hug and a kiss on the cheek.

"Excellent job up there, West." Another voice interrupted their moment. The trio turned their attention to the intruder. Before them stood Rob Cohen, who eagerly shook both Gladys's and Rae's hands. He swept a hand through his blond hair and gave the group an almost blinding smile. Although Rae had just met him, she could see that the smile didn't reach his eyes. Not by a long shot.

"It's great to meet you both. I just wanted to come over and introduce myself and tell Flint that I thought he did a good job out there. Here, I thought you would have been the life of the party, but maybe I was mistaken." His pointed stare at Rae made her raise an eyebrow before narrowing her eyes at him. She hoped her eyes were conveying the thoughts that were running through her mind as she mentally dared him to say something else. As if he understood the look she gave him, he nodded at the group before leaving.

"He was referring to my photo."

"I know. I'll shoot a text message to Rick and Kane and see what they make of it. I know we suspected that he might have been involved before."

"These shenanigans involve him. He chose his words carefully, and no one can tell me otherwise."

"Yeah, but we don't have proof beyond a reasonable doubt." Flint looked up from his phone and into eyes much like his own. "Mom, have you seen Dad?"

"I don't know where your father got off to..." Gladys took a moment to look around for her husband. She soon saw a grin light up Gladys's face, and when Rae turned to look, there was her husband, walking toward her, much like his son had a few moments earlier.

When Terry reached them, he gave his son a firm hug before greeting his wife with a kiss on a cheek and Rae with a grin. "Son, you did a fantastic job up there."

"Thanks, Dad."

"I was wondering if you and Rae wanted to go out to dinner with us tonight? To celebrate your wonderful performance?"

Flint rubbed a hand on the back of his neck. "Can we do a rain check? I don't want to speak for Rae, but I think the adrenaline is wearing off, and I'm pretty beat. Could we do sometime this weekend, if you guys aren't busy?"

Terry looked at Gladys and nodded. "I don't think we're doing anything. Am I missing anything?"

Gladys shook her head before Rae saw the light bulb turn on over her head. "How about we host you guys for dinner at home this weekend?"

Rae gave a slight nod as Flint's hand made its way to the

small of her back. She felt his light tap on her back and glanced up at him. He didn't look all that tired. He and Rae shared a look, and she nodded her head. "That works for us. We'll see you then."

The two couples walked to the entrance of the venue and exchanged pleasantries. It wasn't long before the pairs went their separate ways. Once Rae and Flint were settled into his sedan, she turned to look at him.

"So, are we going to have a quiet night in?"

He threw a glance at her before he turned his attention back to the road. "We'll have a night in, but *quiet* isn't the right word to describe it."

13

———

Rae glanced at her phone when it pinged. That had to be Flint texting her about when he would come over to her apartment for a laid-back movie date night. She glanced at the screen and closed her eyes as a sigh fell from her lips.

Flint: Babe, I can't make it tonight. Got pulled into a last-minute meeting with Rick. Can I make it up to you tomorrow?

The disappointment flowed off of Rae in droves. She wouldn't get to spend time with Flint tonight, but she was also somewhat relieved. Between going to work today and running Flint's town hall event, she was exhausted. Figuring this was a moment where she could relax and have some time for herself, she fired off a message to Flint before tossing her phone down on the coffee table.

Rae: That's fine. I'll see you tomorrow.

She decided this would be a great evening to have a bath. Rae walked into her bathroom and turned the tub faucet on. She watched the water flow down into the tub for a couple of seconds before she turned around and walked to her bathroom counter. She looked up at herself in the mirror and stared at her reflection.

What was she doing? Had she really thought about the implications that Flint's congressional race would have on her? The photo leak was one thing, but being put under a microscope because of the twenty-four-hour news cycle and social media was something else. Was this something she could deal with?

She loved Flint and knew that he would do an amazing job as a congressman. It was something he wanted, and she wanted to do everything in her power to make sure he reached his dreams. Was she giving up too much of herself in the process? Plus, what did she want? She gave herself one last glance in the mirror before turning away to face her tub. Trying to relax while taking a bath was one challenge she had no issues trying to face head-on.

She stripped out of her clothes, put her hair into a high bun, and slid into the bath. Rae was sure everyone in Northern Virginia could hear the sigh she let out. She watched the waves she created and thought about what she wouldn't give to go on another vacation. Her stay in Bermuda a few months ago had been more chaotic than she had liked, even though it had ended with her and Flint talking things out and getting back together. She wanted a vacation that meant no disturbances or distractions for at least a week.

Rae sank lower into the tub, mentally thanking herself for putting her hair into a high bun and not a ponytail. Tackling her hair wasn't something she was prepared to do this evening. Thoughts of the future and what she might want to do flooded her mind. She vowed to take some time tonight to think of some goals she wanted to achieve and focus on what she could do so she could get there.

She finished her bath fifteen minutes later and left the bathroom in her robe. When she figured out which pair of pj's she would wear tonight, she wandered out into her kitchen to grab her glass of wine and her phone. When she had her wine in hand, she walked to the living room, grabbed her phone, and wandered back into her bedroom. She sat down on her bed, reached for her laptop, opened up a new document in her word processor, and stared at the screen. After a few moments of that, she figured her phone would either give her some inspiration or help her procrastinate, so she figured she could have the best of both worlds by checking it.

Flint: Hey, is everything all right?

Flint: Babe?

She noticed the first message was sent right after she sent her message to him before getting into the bath. The second had come about seven minutes ago.

Rae: Yeah, everything is wonderful. Why?

She saw the beloved ellipses pop up on the screen as she waited for Flint to finish his message.

Flint: Just double-checking. Sometimes you say that everything is fine when it's not.

Touché. He wasn't wrong about that.

Rae: No, seriously. Everything is fine. I just got out of the bath, and I'm relaxing at home. No hard feelings about you having to cancel date night.

Flint: You just got out of the bath?

Rae rolled her eyes yet smiled. That was what his mind had zeroed in on.

Rae: *Yes, and you missed it because you had to work. Stay focused, and I'll see you later. Love you.*

She placed the phone next to her and readjusted her positioning, so she felt more prepared for the task at hand.

About half an hour later, she had some solid goals written that she now had to divide into what she wanted to accomplish in the short and long term. They included goals about wanting to buy her own home, finish paying off her student loans, and other places that she wanted to visit. Thoughts about how these goals might entwine with Flint's were put on hold when she looked at her phone and found another message from Flint.

Flint: *Love you too. Have a good rest of your night.*

Rae tossed her phone on her bed and stretched. She reached over to her nightstand and drank the rest of her wine. Her phone pinged again. She was taken aback when her text notification displayed a name she wasn't expecting.

Sarah: *Do you want to get together for coffee tomorrow?*

RAE LOOKED around the cafe until she spotted Sarah sitting near a window across the room from the entrance to the cafe. They had taken a quick break during the workday to grab their coffee together around 2:00 p.m. As she walked up to the table, Sarah looked up and gave her a smile and a wave.

"Thanks for coming out to coffee with me." Rae was immediately drawn to the dark circles that had found a home under Sarah's eyes.

"Sure. It was a great idea to catch up. I didn't know you were back in town."

"Yeah. I've only been back for a few weeks. Spent most of it getting settled and preparing for my new job."

"Oh, really? What are you doing now?"

Sarah took a sip from the water in front of her. "I'm a freelance researcher. I analyze information and provide summaries and feedback for clients. Things have picked up a lot, so I could move back to D.C."

"That's fantastic! Part of my job involves researching now, so I know how time-intensive it can be."

"True, but when you find that diamond in the rough that can help your team or client, it makes it all worth it."

"That's right," Rae said before she asked, "How's your family?" Rae noted the expression that flew across Sarah's face for a millisecond. If she had blinked, the look would have remained a mystery, much like what the weather in D.C. would be on any given day, no matter the season.

Sarah took her time considering the question before she said, "They are okay. Things were rough for a while, but things are now starting to look up."

"That's great! I'm glad things are starting to improve and that you were able to come back to D.C. Are you planning on being in D.C. long term?"

"Everything is kind of in flux, if that makes sense? Would you like a coffee or something else? The menus are right here. I was waiting for you to get here before I ordered." Rae barely got her last comment before Sarah asked her question.

Rae took the menu and glanced over it. Since she was in the mood for a warm chai tea, she placed the menu down and looked back up at Sarah. Sarah offered to order and grab their drinks, so Rae took out her phone to play with until she got back. But Rae had a hard time concentrating on anything on her phone. Something about Sarah's answers wasn't sitting right with her. It was almost as if she was trying to give vague answers on purpose.

Rae looked up from her phone when Sarah returned. "So, are you still with…Mike?" Rae guessed the name of the man that Sarah had been dating while they were living together in D.C. It was one reason she barely saw Sarah when they were living together.

"Yes, that was him. No, we broke up before I left D.C. How's your dating life going?"

"Well, I'm dating Flint again."

Sarah was in the middle of taking a sip of her coffee but paused at Rae's admission. "Oh, really? Did you guys get back together recently?"

"Yes, within the last few months. Things are going well."

"That's great. I'm glad things are working out the second time around. Now that I think about it, I don't think I ever met him."

Rae thought for a moment before she replied, "Yeah, I don't think you have either. Are you dating anyone down here? Maybe we can get together on a double date or something."

"There's a guy I've been talking to and have gone out on a few dates with, but it's not serious. I can see if he wants to go."

"Sounds great. I'll check with Flint, but he's super busy nowadays."

"Oh, really?"

"Yes, he's running for Congress."

"Get out. Your lives must be chaotic."

"Yeah. I'm so proud of him. It's been a lot of work, but it's something he's passionate about, and I want him to succeed, so here we are!" Rae smiled before taking a sip of her tea.

"How does all of it make you feel?"

Rae placed her mug on the table. "What do you mean?" The question took her by surprise. She thought about asking her why she asked the question, but maybe it was just her being paranoid. She bit back the words that threatened to fall from her lips.

"I assume it has to be hard on you. I could only imagine how hectic it is to be running a campaign."

"True, but he also has help. His team has been fantastic." Rae held back a comment about how she didn't particularly like Rick because badmouthing Flint's campaign manager wouldn't be a good look. That didn't negate the fact that Rick had been very good at his job besides nitpicking at Rae.

"That's great. I'll look more into his race. I could only imagine what life is like for you with your significant other running for office."

"Yeah, well...it can be tough, but I wouldn't change it for anything. He's doing something he loves, and I want to support him."

"Doesn't mean it's not hard on you, though."

"But isn't that life? Especially when you're working toward goals that you want to accomplish?"

Sarah's shoulders reached her ears as if to say "good point." Rae's statement changed the topic, and the two spent another thirty minutes talking before they left the cafe.

"It was great getting to see you again."

"Likewise. We should get together again soon. And I'll let you know about that double date."

"Sounds good. See you soon." With that, Rae headed to the metro to go back to her job without a second thought.

14

———

Rae reached her apartment pretty quickly and opened her front door. She closed the door, hung up her coat, and took off her boots before checking her phone.

Liv: Anyone want to get together for movie night tonight? I know it's last minute and a work night, but I'm bored. Just staying in though cause who wants to dress to go out and we haven't gotten together in a while.

Rae: I'm down.

Eve: Sounds like a plan.

Jules: I can make it.

Liv: Great. I'll host. How about 7 p.m.?

Rae sent the thumbs-up emoji before checking the time. She had about an hour to burn before heading over to Liv's. She ended up starting a load of laundry before her phone pinged.

Flint: Hey, beautiful. How's it going? How did coffee go with Sarah?

Rae smiled at Flint's thoughtful message. Although the

compliment was sweet, it somewhat surprised her that he remembered her coffee date with Sarah.

Rae: It went well! She's living in the area somewhere and seems to be doing well. She has only been back in town for a few weeks. I brought up us going on a double date sometime soon with a guy she is seeing.

Flint: Sounds interesting. I'm not sure how busy they are, but I can throw out some dates that should work for me if that's easier.

Rae thought that made sense since Flint was probably the busiest out of everyone, although she didn't know for sure.

Rae: Perfect. Just send them over. Anyway, how's your day going?

Flint: Busy. We've been hopping from event to event. Ready to be done and spend some time with you. Are you busy this evening?

Rae: Yeah, I made plans with the girls to have a movie night, but I can head over to your apartment after?

Flint: Perfect. Do you want to stay over tomorrow night as well? I have nothing going on tomorrow. You could leave from here to go to work.

Rae waited a few minutes to reply while she finished washing dishes.

Rae: Maybe.

RAE DROPPED her small duffel bag next to her as she settled in at Liv's place. The eccentrically decorated apartment fit her friend perfectly. Eve walked past her and sat on the couch. The two friends had just arrived at Liv's apartment, and all three were waiting on Jules.

Liv raised an eyebrow at her before putting the wineglasses she was carrying down on her coffee table. "Going somewhere?"

"You mean travel-wise?" Liv nodded her head. "I wish. I'm headed over to Flint's after this. Figured it would be nice to have another set of clothes instead of the clothes I've left over there."

"You know you wouldn't have to bring clothes over to his house if you already lived there." Rae threw a small pillow at Liv, who stuck her tongue out in return. "You know I'm just messing around."

"I know, but it's also something I've been thinking about. Flint briefly mentioned it, and I probably wouldn't do it until my lease ran out."

Eve looked up from her position on the couch. "You're serious."

"I am. I don't want to do it now with everything going on with the campaign, but I've been tossing the thought around in my head."

"That makes sense. It's not a straightforward decision to make, plus his campaign is already a huge, life-altering event. Don't want the added stress of moving in together right now."

"Yeah, it will be a lot besides having to break my lease, and then we would have to decide if I would move into his apartment or if we would find a new apartment together, which might mean breaking another lease."

There was a knock on the door that halted the conversation. Liv moved toward the door and opened it, letting Jules inside.

"Hey, ladies. What did I miss?"

"Nothing much. Rae was just telling us about how she was thinking about moving in with Flint."

"Oh, really? That's great!" Jules took off her coat and walked over to Liv's closet. "I assume if you did, you'll stay near your current apartment because it would be in his soon-to-be district."

Rae smiled at Jules's confidence that Flint would win the race.

"Probably. I was telling these two we haven't really talked about it in depth yet. Just a casual mention of it here and there. Speaking of moving apartments, I met up with Sarah today."

"Sarah..." Rae could see that Liv was having a hard time putting a face to the name.

"My old roommate, Sarah."

No one said anything for a second before Jules chimed in. "How is she doing? I thought you mentioned she moved back to her hometown when you guys moved out of the apartment you shared."

"She did, apparently, but she's back now as of a few weeks ago. She ran into me when I was grabbing lunch with my mom. We got caught up today."

"Is she still dating that one guy? I remember she was never around, and so we ended up having free rein over your apartment most of the time." Eve leaned forward to grab her glass of wine.

Rae gave them a rundown of what had happened during her coffee outing with Sarah. "It was nice to catch up and see that she's doing well. I do find it a little weird that she is all of a sudden back in town, but stranger things have happened." Her mother's words about coincidences floated back into her mind. There wasn't any way she could prove that something suspicious was afoot with Sarah's reappearance or questions, but she couldn't shake the feeling.

"Anyway, it's also nice to be here with y'all. Today feels like I'm having a bit of a break from all the mayhem that's been Flint's congressional race and this photo leak."

"Any progress on that front?" Liv asked as she headed to her kitchen. She quickly returned with another wineglass and poured the wine that she had set out earlier.

"A little. We talked to Kane the other day." Rae threw a glance over at Eve to see her reaction to his name. She had picked up on something being amiss the few times that Eve and Kane had been in the same room with one another. Eve's eye twitched before she rubbed it, and Rae smirked. "He did some digging and said that it had to have come from someone who either took the original photo, which would be Eve, or snatched it off my social media pages. It was only one social media site, and I have locked down my page like Fort Knox, so it was more than likely someone either Eve or I am connected to who leaked the photo. Side note, Eve, what is up with you and Kane?"

Rae watched as Eve's eyes narrowed down into a glare. "What do you mean, what's up with us?"

"You started acting weird when he's around."

"No, I don't."

"Yes, you do."

"Nope." Eve put her wineglass back on the coffee table and leaned back, arms crossed over her body.

"You don't have to tell us if you don't want to."

"But we know you do," Liv chimed in from the peanut gallery.

Eve rolled her eyes and replied, "Fine. Kane and I went on one date just after Flint moved to Colorado, all right?"

Everyone looked at Eve with a shocked expression on their faces. Liv was the first to recover. "You went out on a date with Kane and didn't tell us?!"

"Yep, because he told me it wouldn't work out after that date. So, I kept it to myself." Eve sighed and ran a hand through her short, dark locks. "I didn't want to embarrass myself further, okay?"

Rae leaned over and put an arm around her shoulder. "I'm sorry I pushed you to share what happened."

"It's fine. Honestly, it feels better to get it out. Plus, it happened years ago. It's awkward now."

"Good. And now we have permission to whip his ass."

The women could always count on Liv to provide some comedic relief.

"And without further ado, let's get this movie started."

While Liv found *Bridesmaids*, Eve whispered in Rae's ear, "Would next week work for you and Flint? To start interviewing you guys?"

Rae pulled on her ponytail as she thought about Eve's comment before flipping her hair over her shoulder.

"Sounds like a plan."

RAE DASHED into the front lobby of Flint's apartment building. It had started snowing while she was in the cab to Flint's house, and she hadn't brought an umbrella. She waved at the front desk person before she pressed the button to summon the elevator. Thankfully, the elevator came in just a few seconds, and she was on Flint's floor in record time. Rae adjusted the strap of her overnight bag as she walked toward Flint's front door. Before she knocked, the door swung open.

"Hey, babe."

"Hey, yourself," Rae said as Flint moved aside to let her into his apartment.

"Do you need a towel or anything? I saw that it started raining. Let me take that for you." He grabbed her bag before gesturing to his window that had splatters of snow crystals on it.

"I'm good. I stepped out of the cab and almost immediately into your lobby. So, I'm mostly dry." Rae took off the hoodie she had sported while she was outside.

Flint paused for a second. "I would make a dirty joke, but I think I'll keep it to myself."

Rae shook her head with a smile. "You forgot to do something."

"Oh?"

"This." She leaned up and kissed him.

When they broke apart, Flint said, "I missed that."

"Me too."

"How was your day?"

"Good. I had to—" A strange sound rang from Flint's phone.

"Did you add a special ringtone to Rick's contact to warn you when he was calling? I mean, I would have."

Flint shook his head before reading something on his phone. "Nope. Apparently, it's an alert that because of the incoming snowstorm, the city is shutting down."

15

———

"I forgot about the snowstorm that was supposed to be coming. And I'm a little annoyed that you were the only one who got that alert sent to your phone." Rae heard Flint chuckle at her words, but she didn't acknowledge him. "I can't remember the last time we had snow at this time of year."

She stared out at the flurries as they made their way past the window. The sight relaxed her as she took another sip from the coffee she had been nursing for the last couple of minutes.

"I know. Apparently, the predictions are right on the money, and this storm will be bad." Flint walked up behind Rae and placed his hands around her waist as he joined her to watch the snow fall.

"Well, the D.C. area closes down at the sight of a flurry, so I don't blame them for shutting down early if what the meteorologists are predicting comes true."

Flint chuckled. "You're not wrong."

Rae turned her head to look at him over her shoulder. His arms around her provided a sense of comfort that she hadn't realized she wanted right now. She would pay good money for them to go back to bed and snuggle up together.

"You know we can't do that right now. Although it is something I'd love to do too."

"Huh?"

"You said that you wanted to go back to bed and snuggle."

Her cheeks heated as she realized she made a mistake and said her thoughts out loud.

"Too bad today is Thursday, and we have to work."

"True. But if the snowstorm is as bad as they think, chances are we'll be working remotely tomorrow as well, and then we have the weekend."

Rae paused before she said, "You're not wrong." She couldn't stop the smile from forming on her lips.

"I know."

Rae shook her head at Flint as she placed one of her hands over his. She turned her body toward his and rubbed a hand up and down his sweater-covered chest. She then stood up on her tiptoes to meet his lips with a kiss. Rae took a step back when Flint tried to make the kiss more intense.

"I thought you said we can't do that right now?"

"That was before you started rubbing your hand up and down my chest."

Rae burst out laughing and shook her head at Flint once more.

"We should probably get to work." She stepped out of his embrace and strolled over to Flint's dining room table, where they had set up a makeshift office. Flint had a spare room in his apartment that he was using as both a guest room and an office, but there wasn't enough room for both of them to be in there at the same time. Rae sat down in a chair and turned on her laptop.

Flint made his way past the dining room as he headed toward the kitchen. "Do you want anything to eat? I think I could find something to whip up quickly, given all the food that we have."

Rae rolled her eyes. They hadn't bought that much food. Just enough to get through two to three days without needing to order delivery. "A bagel and cream cheese would be great."

"That's what I was thinking. Do you want anything else? More coffee? Water."

Rae thought for a moment. "Water would be amazing."

"Coming right up."

Rae took a second to stretch as she gathered her thoughts about what she wanted to accomplish today and could do so easily from home. She pulled up her to-do list on her computer to type it out.

"So, I have a meeting in an hour to check in with Danielle. There might be one other call that I'm not sure is happening because I'm not sure if that organization is working from home too." She made a note to check in with her contact there ahead of the potential call.

"I have calls on and off all day today, so I'll probably just take those in my office, so I don't disturb you." Flint placed a bagel and water in front of her before heading back into the kitchen.

"I know I don't have to say this, but you can go work in your office. I'm fine with working out here."

"Don't worry about it. Plus, I'll be getting exercise walking to and from the dining room."

Rae giggled. She was sure Flint went to the gym in the basement of his apartment building this morning before she was fully awake to realize it.

Flint came back into the dining room with a bagel of his own and a coffee. He placed them in front of the seat he had chosen, diagonally across from Rae. She watched as he headed toward his office and his bedroom. He soon emerged with his laptop and their cell phones.

"Thanks," said Rae, when Flint handed over her phone. Finding nothing pressing on it, she set it facedown on the table and got ready to work.

A few hours later, Rae stood up and stretched her limbs. After sitting down on a hard chair for several hours, her body direly needed some movement that didn't involve typing a bunch of things on a keyboard. She grabbed her water bottle and headed to the kitchen for a refill. She walked back to her computer, placing the refilled water bottle down in front of her before she debated what to do next. Flint had left the room to take a call while she had been on a video conference call with Danielle. She could hear him talking from his office, so who knew when he would reappear. She sat at her makeshift desk for a few moments to figure out what she should do next. When her stomach growled, she had her answer.

She walked into the kitchen to figure out what she could throw together that would give her enough time to eat before having to tackle more tasks for work. Rae decided on a beef stir fry was her best bet.

"Something smells great."

Rae looked over her shoulder and smiled at Flint before

turning her attention back to the food in the pan. "I'm glad. How'd your meetings go?"

"Not too bad. We had another meeting about your leaked photos."

Rae stopped stirring and sighed. "What happened?"

Flint brushed a hand through his hair as he walked around Rae and leaned back on the countertop to the right of her. She could feel his eyes staring at her. Something bad had to have happened on the call.

"Flint, what happened?" Rae asked again.

Flint sighed. "Well, the good news is that no more pictures have leaked. And Rick mentioned that he thought you were doing great at keeping a low profile. That maybe this would work after all."

Rae's hand clutched the wooden spatula she was holding so tightly that she wondered if she had the ability to break it. The fact that she was doing any of this was a sore subject. "What is this? Does he mean our relationship?" Rae saw red. "I—"

"Wait, let me finish. I told him that there was no way that this wouldn't work and that if he even alluded to us having to break up, I would fire him."

Rae slowly nodded her head as she digested what Flint said. Although she wanted to, she knew it would be childish to gloat.

"Rae, I'll do everything in my power to find out who leaked those photos of you. And they'll have to answer for it." Flint's reply and the look in his eye sent a shiver down Rae's spine. Her attention shifted back to the pan of food she was making, but her stirring became erratic. She could feel a headache forming that she knew would be a pain to get rid of.

"I can also handle this myself."

Flint gently removed the spatula from her hand. When she protested, he gave her a small smile. "I'm sure the stir-fry won't burn that fast. I know you can handle this yourself, but you wouldn't be in this situation if it weren't for me running for office. It's not fair to you, and I want to do everything in my power to take whoever is doing this down. This doesn't mean that I'm taking over the situation completely, and you can tell me to back off at any point. I also won't do anything without telling you. We're a team."

Those words helped relieve some tension that was forming in her head. She nodded as she grabbed the wooden spatula and began stirring again. "Do you have any suggestions about what to do next?"

"I think we need to enlist Kane's help again. He didn't do as much to help us last time around because things...snowballed out of control. I already had him digging into this a bit, but hadn't mentioned bringing him on in an official capacity."

Rae didn't want to think about the events that occurred a few months ago that had led to their brief breakup. "Bringing Kane would work. And we know that he would keep things quiet, which would be important for your campaign. Would you have to pay him for it? And would that mean it would have to come out of campaign funds, or is it something you could pay for personally? Hell, I guess I could pay for it personally."

"Knowing Kane, he'll do it for free, but that's an excellent point. Let me see when he is available to talk." Flint started typing a message out on his phone before pausing. "Do you need me to help with lunch? I can do that first and then reach out to Kane."

Rae smiled before shaking her head. "I think I have a good handle on lunch. You connect with Kane and see what our options are."

"I'll be right back." Flint leaned over to give her a kiss on her forehead before heading out of the room to call Kane.

By the time Rae was placing their lunch on the dining room table, Flint had walked back into the room. "Any word from Kane?"

"Yes. He's available to talk this evening. He thinks he might have a small lead, so he wanted to do a bit of digging beforehand to provide us with some information on the call."

"Sounds good. Let's hope today doesn't bring any more drama."

And the rest of the day flew by with minimal distraction on Rae's end. The standing call that she was hoping would get canceled did, and she spent most of her time working on policy briefs and answering emails from her colleagues and other partner organizations. She watched Flint float in and out of the room, based on whether he was taking a call or returning from one. Now that it was the end of the workday, she'd hoped that she would have Flint all to herself. Well, besides the call with Kane. And if Rick called or texted, she assumed he would have to answer those too.

Flint walked back into the dining room just as Rae was closing her laptop.

"What do you want for dinner?"

Flint thought for a second and smiled. "How about I whip

something up, and you sit here and enjoy a glass of wine on the house?"

Rae chuckled before replying, "You had a busier day than I did. I'm happy to fix dinner. But I'll take that glass of wine no matter what."

"No, you had a longer day than I did. I'm happy to fix dinner."

"That works. Plus, who knows what type of news we will hear from Kane. I'm happy to fix dinner."

Rae couldn't believe they were arguing over who should fix dinner, but he had a point. Who knew what information they would hear from Kane. Taking his words into consideration, Rae conceded.

"Fine, you can start with dinner, and I want a glass of wine. I can be sous chef if you want me to be. Or I can just sit on the countertop and keep you company."

"That works."

RAE PLACED her hands on her belly as she tried to recover from all the food she had just eaten. And she had no regrets.

"I have appointed you head chef from now on."

Flint laughed at Rae's proclamation. "You still have me beat, hands down."

"I don't know, babe. That baked chicken was delicious."

"I'm glad."

"I would kiss you, but I think it would require too much effort to lean over."

Flint shook his head as he reached for his phone. "Should I see if Kane is available to talk now?"

Flint's question took the radiant energy out of the room. Not that Rae blamed him for asking, but she didn't know if she was ready to face this head-on yet. She took a few deep breaths before nodding her head. "Sure. Might as well rip the Band-Aid off." She watched as Flint called Kane and could hear her heart thumping in her chest. Rae didn't know why she was this nervous. Maybe it had to do with the fact that she had no idea what would be revealed on the other end of this call.

"Are you okay?"

Rae shook her head to clear her thoughts. She hadn't realized that she had been daydreaming until Flint's words brought her back to reality. "Yeah, I'm fine. Why?"

"'Cause you are clenching that pillow as if you're holding on for dear life." Flint gestured to one pillow on his couch that she hadn't even realized she had been touching, let alone holding onto tightly.

"I'm okay. Just got lost in my thoughts, that's all."

"Wanna talk about it? I didn't start the call with Kane yet."

She took another deep breath in before slowly letting it out. "I just...don't know how to feel about this call."

"What do you mean?"

Rae bit her bottom lip before she said, "I guess I'm nervous about what we may or may not find out."

Flint paused for a moment before leaning over and taking hold of both of her hands. "I'm frightened about what we might learn too, but we're doing this to protect you and to get justice. You've had a lot to deal with over the last few months, and although we thought this was wrapped up months ago, it wasn't. Now whether or not this is related to the stunts that the Hopkinses pulled on us, I don't know. But whoever this is isn't just going to walk all over us without consequences, okay? You aren't alone in this fight. I love you, and we'll face this together."

Rae smiled before sitting back down. She handed Flint his phone and said, "Make the call."

16

"Hey, man. How's it going?"

"Fine besides...you know what. Rae is here."

"Hey, Rae, I'm asking the obvious even though I can probably figure out the answer. How's it going?"

"Could be worse."

"That's true, ain't it? Getting right to the chase, Flint brought me up to speed on everything that has gone down since we chatted last. At least the photo isn't being talked about nearly as much as it was."

"Thanks for that reminder." The sarcasm dripping off of Flint's words made Rae side-eye him as she waited for Kane to respond. "Do you have anything for us to go on? I know it's been a bit since the photo leaked."

"I have something, but I'm not sure how helpful it is."

Rae's stomach traveled up to her throat, where she was sure it had found a comfortable spot to sit.

Flint reached over and held Rae's hand. "Go on."

"Rae, you locked your social media accounts down, right?"

Rae nodded her head. "Yeah, I got paranoid about it a few years back when I was searching for jobs. I deleted some photos, untagged myself in others, and tried to make my account more secure, etc. I caught myself increasing my privacy and security settings even more after this photo leak happened."

"But everyone knows that once something is on the internet, it's essentially there forever."

"Kane, what did you find?" Rae glanced over at Flint, noting the seriousness in his tone. His hand gently stroked hers, giving her a little comfort when her nerves couldn't take where this conversation was going.

"So, I think the person who snatched that photo of you must be some connection to you on whichever social media account the photo was on. The other option is that they snatched it before you updated your privacy settings, but that would mean they were holding on to that photo and potentially others for years."

And that was when the floor opened up and swallowed Rae whole. She looked to Flint again because she didn't know how to react.

"So, chances are that it's someone that Rae knows."

"Unless you got hacked, Rae, which I assume you didn't, or this person spent days tracking you and some acquaintances from your past, I would assume the person who had access to your photos is someone you've known for quite a while. Possibly downloaded the photos before you increased the privacy settings and untagged yourself. Now, this isn't saying that there aren't other ways to do this, just that this is probably how I would have done it."

"How you would have done it, huh?" The tension in the room decreased when Rae saw the smirk on Flint's face.

"You know what I mean. Now I might find out who the person is, but it'll take some time."

"Sounds good. Thanks for the quick update."

"Yes, thanks, Kane. If there's anything you need from us, let us know."

"You got it. But I know you guys have a lot on your plate, so I won't bug you unless it's something big."

"Thanks, man."

"Wait." Rae rushed to say before they hung up. "I feel like an idiot for asking this now, but why are we going to Kane with this? And Kane, how are you so...well-versed in this?"

Once again, silence took hold of the room. Rae didn't think Flint realized that his pursed lips were telling her that there was a bigger story here than he was letting on. A sliver of his tongue appeared, and he ran it across his lips.

"Kane, I'll let you speak for yourself."

"Ahem."

Rae flipped her hair over one shoulder and raised an eyebrow at Flint as she waited for Kane to finish clearing his throat. Flint's face was still blank, besides his lips sitting in a thin line across his face.

"Let's just say I work in the security field. A lot of the aspects of my job outside of the foundation I can't talk about."

"So, you do that outside of heading the foundation?" Rae referenced the foundation that he and Flint had cofounded to help combat veteran homelessness.

"Yes." Rae waited a beat, but Kane didn't offer up anything

else, effectively ending the conversation. The couple spent a few more seconds saying goodbye to their friend before Flint hung up the phone.

"Wow," said Rae as she replayed certain segments of the conversation in her mind. "Not only is this situation a mess, but you have some very interesting friends."

"Let's get Kane's 'job' out of the way first. I'm not even sure if I know all that he does. To be frank, he's not lying about not being able to talk about his job. And that wasn't his way of trying to get out of talking to you about it. I don't know a lot about what he does outside of his role at Homes for Vets. But I trust his judgment with both the foundation and helping us out here."

"Huh." Rae pulled at her hair, putting it into a makeshift ponytail before she sighed. "Changing the subject here, where the hell do we begin with what he said about our social media accounts?"

Flint sat back but said nothing. "How many connections do you have on social media?"

All Rae did was stare at Flint. "Over 1,000? If you count all of my accounts? I don't post on them much, though."

Flint was quiet again. After a few more moments of silence, Rae couldn't take it anymore. "So, should I take a deep dive and look through my friends list to see who might have a grudge against me and want to leak photos from eight to ten years ago?"

"That's probably not a good use of your time unless you know for a fact that someone doesn't like you."

"Great point. But now what?"

"I'm not sure." Flint rubbed the back of his neck before he scooted over a bit to wrap his arm around Rae.

She laid her head down on his shoulder, and the silence that surrounded them calmed her, in a way. There wasn't really anything anyone could do or say. She never imagined that an old acquaintance could have potentially sold her out because her boyfriend was entering the political fray. But maybe that was naïve of her.

"Hey, I think it's snowing again."

Rae glanced out of the window at Flint's words. She got up and wandered over to the window. He was right. She could see the flurries dashing down under the street lamp near Flint's apartment. She felt Flint's presence behind her before she heard him.

"You know, this is how we began the morning. I loved that."

"I did too," she whispered.

"What if we make this a permanent thing?"

Rae turned her head and looked up at him. "What?"

Flint's gaze turned more serious as he stared down into her eyes, then to her lips, before migrating back up to her eyes. "I wanted to discuss moving in together. We don't have to stay here either. We can find a new apartment and move into that one together. And this isn't me asking you like a proposal, but I wanted to know how you felt about it and—"

At first, Rae was speechless. Sure, the thought had crossed her mind, outside of the fact that she and her friends had talked about it somewhat recently. But she hadn't thought the option was on the table.

Then she smiled. She could tell that Flint was nervous about asking her even though he hadn't really asked her. Had he? "I'm happy to have a discussion about it. I loved our moment this morning. And I love the one we're having right now."

"Well, whenever you want to have that discussion, I'm right here." The words flew out of Flint's mouth, which made Rae laugh.

"You're nervous, aren't you? It's okay. It's not like you asked me to marry you. That would be downright terrifying." Rae nudged him with her head before giggling once more.

"I guess I was nervous about it. I had been thinking about it for a bit. Ever since the campaign ramped up and the only time we could spend together was if one of us went to the other's apartment after a long day. But I didn't want that to be the reason we moved in together. That is, if you agreed."

"That makes sense. Let's table this conversation for right now and pick this up when we both aren't exhausted, nor have a million things floating through our minds. Or I could just be speaking for myself because that conversation with Kane...was a lot."

"I shouldn't have brought up moving in together right after that conversation. You're dealing with enough right now, and I just added something else to your plate."

Rae slid out of Flint's embrace and turned around to face him, much like she had that morning.

"Don't worry about it. The thought was already on my mind. I just wasn't prepared to discuss it right now."

"I'm sorry—"

Rae placed a hand on Flint's chest. "I swear, it's fine. Let's just talk about it at another time. We should probably get to cleaning up the mess we made from dinner."

"Sounds like a plan."

As Rae was gathering the dishes from the dining room

table, she fought the urge to think about the discussion that Flint wanted to have about them moving in together. He was ready to take the next step, but was she? Plus, none of this solved the main issue at hand. Who leaked the photo to the press?

17

"This snow is testing my patience."

"Being forced to stay in one place is annoying, but I think we've been doing pretty well together." He paused. "Don't you think so?"

Rae turned her body toward Flint's but said nothing. The couple was in bed after another evening of being shut in because of the snowstorm that was still raging on and off in the Washington, D.C. metro area. She swallowed a laugh that was on the back of her throat. "I mean, it hasn't been bad."

Flint's eyes widened, and Rae couldn't hide her laughter any longer. Flint's eyes narrowed as Rae laughed, looked at him again, and then laughed even harder.

"I was just kidding." The words rushed out between the laughter she couldn't control. "The look on your face was priceless." Rae wiped her watery eyes as she tried to stop the giggles that slipped from her mouth. "Whew."

Once Rae pulled herself together, she placed a hand on Flint's cheek and said, "I've enjoyed spending all of this time with you. We went from hardly seeing each other to spending several days together." She tossed a piece of hair that had fallen into her face back over her shoulder. "And we've only had one minor argument."

Flint huffed. "You didn't win that game."

Rae chuckled at his reference to the board game they played earlier. "I did."

"You didn't."

Rae removed her hand. "I did, and you know it."

"You didn't because you cheated."

Rae cleared her throat. "I distinctly remember you saying that you couldn't believe that I pulled that move and that it was a game-changer."

Flint sighed. "It's better to play Monopoly with more people, anyway."

"I won't deny that. We should have a board game night once this weather clears up."

"That wasn't what I was getting at, though."

Rae noted the change in the tone of his voice. The teasing, fake argumentative tone was gone, and his voice grew lower, telling her that what he was about to say was more serious.

"I wanted to get your thoughts on us moving in together."

Rae knew the double-take she just did had to have been comical. "Um. Okay. Wasn't expecting that."

"You don't sound too thrilled to—"

"No, no. Flint, this is something we should talk about."

Rae could feel Flint's eyes studying her, but he said nothing. There was a sense of awkwardness that floated between the couple, which she assumed was because he hadn't been expecting that answer. Flint's lack of a response was getting to her until she couldn't take it anymore.

"Flint, I think this would be the next step in our relationship, and I'm partially excited about taking that step. But I also want it to be under the right conditions."

"What do you mean, right conditions?"

Rae debated how she should say what she wanted to say. "Flint, we have so many things going on right now. You're running for Congress, and that has our lives in a tailspin, and we have someone who doesn't want you running for Congress. This is coming after all the drama with the Hopkinses and your mom, granted the latter have both been quiet, and your mom has been helpful since the colossal blowup. But that's a big decision to make when we are getting pulled in different directions. I don't want the reason that we move in together to be because we wanted to see each other more or to have our judgment clouded by everything else that is going on." Rae saw the expression on Flint's face and shook her head at herself. "I'm fucking this up."

"No, I think I get it. This isn't the right time to talk about it."

"I'm not saying that. I'm happy you brought it up as the thought crossed my mind a few times more recently." That brought a slight smile to Flint's face. "I think us talking this out makes sense. But I would like time to think it over before coming to a concrete decision."

"I understand that. Can I tell you my thoughts on it?"

Rae nodded and said, "Sure. You know I always want to hear what you're thinking."

"I'd want to move in with you if we had no stress or if we had all the stress in the world. But I also understand what you're saying, and I'm okay with us talking about it more until you can reach a decision."

"Thank you," Rae said. Flint pulled her into a hug and then fell backward, pulling Rae with him. They both landed on the bed with a small thump and Rae ended up on top of Flint. She let out another giggle as she looked down into Flint's eyes.

"I love your laughter even when it's at my expense."

"I'm glad because most of the time I'm laughing at you, not with you."

Flint snorted as Rae leaned down and gave him a small peck on the lips.

"You know I'm just kidding."

"Are you? I think you've been hanging out with Liv too much. That sounded like something she would say."

"Yeah, it did." Rae leaned down and gave him another quick kiss on his lips. This time, the smile turned into a full-blown grin.

"Do you want to keep talking about moving in together, or do you want to table it for now?"

"How about we table it again and talk about it later? I have the feeling that you probably want to do something else at the moment." Rae emphasized the word *feeling*. "I can help you out with that."

"Oh, really?" Rae laughed as Flint took off her tank top and flipped them over. "I'd prefer to help you out."

The moan that fell from his lips once their lips touched was anything but quiet. He moved to her neck and lightly sucked, causing goosebumps to appear on her skin. Flint left a line of kisses down her collarbone and onto her shoulder, sending even more shivers throughout her body. Rae sighed in contentment. Her neck had always been sensitive, and he was using it to her advantage.

"You know, I'll never get tired of seeing this necklace against your skin." He briefly played with it before kissing around the piece of jewelry as he made his way toward her chest. Her nipples grew hard like tiny pebbles when he cupped her breasts. She was ecstatic that there hadn't been a need for her to wear a bra in days, and there was one less barrier between her and Flint. Another point to team *snatch off bras as soon as you get home*, because they're uncomfortable as all get out. When he rolled her nipple between his thumb and index finger, it sent shock waves that felt like a tsunami down to her toes. He alternated between these motions, sending her body into overdrive before his hands headed south.

His fingers made their way down her body, leaving a trail of touches that soon his mouth followed up with kisses. When his hands reached her thighs, he slowly peeled away her panties, and Rae growled.

"You're doing this on purpose."

"What could have possibly given you that idea?"

Rae's eyes stopped mid-roll, and a gasp fell from her lips when his mouth touched her. Although she knew his mouth was busy, she could still hear him snickering. By the time Flint stopped, Rae was ready to shoot off like a rocket. When he slowly slid into her, he set off a chain reaction in her body. As she was riding out her orgasm, he sped up his tempo and added his fingers to the mix. He continued at the same pace until they both went over the edge, his moan joining hers as they reached their highest peak.

As they were coming down from their climaxes, Flint laid

his head on her breasts and said, "I could die right here, right now, and be happy."

Those words led Rae to belly laugh. "How do you even come up with these things? You should be exhausted."

Flint looked up from his position and gave Rae a boyish grin. "I wish I knew."

"I think D.C. will open up tomorrow."

Rae looked up from the book she was reading and glanced at Flint. It was the next evening, and Flint was still working on his laptop. Although it was past the time Flint had told her he would stop working, Rae said nothing. She had finished her work for the day and pulled out a book she had brought to Flint's apartment after they decided they would stay there until everything reopened.

Rae stretched before picking at the ends of her long brown ponytail. "Doesn't make much of a difference to me, personally. I still can't go into the office."

She assumed her words grabbed Flint's attention because his eyes moved from his laptop screen to her. "I'm so sorry that you're still home dealing with this crap."

"Any word from Kane?"

Flint shook his head. "I'll shoot him a message to see if he has any updates."

Rae didn't respond. Her mind had wandered off into a daydream. She came to when she heard Flint call her name. "Huh?"

"I lost you there."

"Yeah, I know. Lost in another daydream."

"Want to share?"

Flint's question caused the butterflies that Rae hadn't realized were there to dance in her stomach. "It's weird."

"So? I always want to hear what you're thinking."

Rae smirked. "That's a lie."

"No, it's not. I'm always curious about things that matter to you. So, if you want to tell me what's up, feel free."

Rae played with the ends of her ponytail as she thought of a way to say what she was thinking. "You know how we talked about moving in together?"

"Yes." Flint moved his laptop to the coffee table and turned his attention to her.

"And I'm hesitant to do that." *Shit.* "I mean, I'm hesitant to make that decision right now."

Rae saw that Flint's eyes never left her face. That made Rae's heart pound faster because of what she was about to say.

"How about we exchange keys? Well, I guess it would be me giving you my key since I already know the code to your front door. That's a step forward, right? Then discuss moving in together after the election?"

"You have yourself a deal, Ms. Carter." Flint stuck his hand out to shake Rae's. She chuckled at Flint's actions before sticking her hand out too. She smiled when he gave her a firm handshake and turned his hand so that the back of hers was facing up. He then leaned down to kiss it before placing her hand back in her lap.

"You're a trip."

"Haven't heard that saying in a while."

"I'm a walking throwback." Rae stood up and stretched. "I

should probably get to working on dinner. I volunteered to do it tonight."

"Do you want any company?"

His question startled Rae. Usually, Flint spent just about every waking moment working on either something related to work or his campaign. "You don't have something to do for work?"

Flint leaned over and looked at his laptop before standing up. "I see nothing from Rick or Kate, so it looks like I might be free." He brushed his hands along his thighs and took a step toward Rae. "Do you need a sous chef?"

"I'll always need you as my sous chef. Come on. We should get the food started before it gets too late."

18

———

That weekend, the snow finally stopped, and the D.C. metropolitan area dug its way out. Businesses were reopening this weekend, which made Rae happy, but she was also grateful to have this time spent with Flint with few distractions.

He pulled his phone out of his back pocket and studied the screen for a moment.

Rae couldn't hide her disdain and rolled her eyes. "I swear if that is Rick calling you after nine on a Saturday night, I'll—"

"It's Kane."

"Oh."

Flint answered the call and said, "Hey, man. Give me a second. Let me put you on speaker since Rae is here."

Rae followed Flint over to his couch, where he placed his phone down on the coffee table. "Kane, you're on speaker-phone. What's up?"

"Hey, I'm glad you're both together. That makes this easier."

"What do you mean, easier?"

"I heard some intel that someone was trying to dig up some dirt on you guys."

"That's not shocking, though, right?" Rae looked at Flint before looking back at the phone. "Opponents would want to dig up dirt on Flint. It would make for a great ad to play in front of voters. At least that has been my experience working for different organizations."

"Yes, and I'm sure that your own campaign has done some digging of their own into your backgrounds." Rae nodded her head, although Kane couldn't see her. Rick had admitted that they had. "This is deeper than that. They are going for blood. Flint, do you remember Carl?"

"Vaguely, but we didn't do many things together."

"Right, he and I hung out more than you and he did. Someone asked him about you online. Did it in a roundabout way, but they did. Carl didn't give up any information, but he called and let me know because he knew you and I were good friends."

"I'm glad he said nothing."

Rae didn't know her mouth was agape until she closed it. "Is it right to assume then, that the leaking of the photo of me from college wasn't a one-off thing? Like someone is trying to tear the campaign down by leaking embarrassing things about us?"

"Right. And I would assume they're just getting started. Which means we need to find out who this is, and fast. Because who knows what information they have and how they got it. Or what other information they could get."

"What can we do?"

"Well, Carl gave me the username of the person who tried

to contact him, so I'm doing everything in my power to find out who that person is. I assume you've already done this since you both added more security to your social media accounts, but I would also suggest changing any passwords to any accounts you use. Add two-factor identification or extra security measures, if you haven't. I'm tracking what I can online, but who knows when whoever this is will strike."

"Can we get the police involved?"

"I mean, you can talk to them, but chances are they can't do anything right now because technically the person or people have done nothing wrong. The photo that was leaked was on social media, so it was fair game."

Rae's hands flew up to her face. She felt Flint wrap his arm around her and rub small circles on her arm.

"If I hear anything else, I'll let y'all know. I'm sorry I don't have more positive news."

"It's fine, man. You're doing everything you can do to help us here."

"I'll talk to you all later. Hopefully, something pops."

With that, Kane hung up. Flint pulled Rae into his arms and rubbed her back as the two sat in silence, digesting the information. A few moments passed before Rae pulled back and looked Flint in the eye.

"We need to figure out our next move. We know more than likely, this person will strike again. The only thing we don't know is how." Rae moved out of Flint's grasp and stood up. She walked back and forth as she tried to come up with a solution to the problem at hand. "Should we scour through our social media contacts? Maybe Kane can help with that."

"Honestly, that might be our only option. I think we also need to find out if this person is trying to hurt me by going through you or trying to hurt you and is trying to take the campaign down with it."

"What if it's both?"

"You mean that someone wants to take us both down?"

Flint nodded his head.

"I don't know about you, but I can't think of anyone that would have a vendetta against—"

Rae stopped pacing to look at Flint. "Are we thinking of the same people?"

"Probably."

"But what would Calvin and Marie Hopkins gain from any of this now? Okay, I'm sure confronting them a few months ago and them having to air some of their dirty laundry. It's not like they got banished to the ends of the earth."

"To you, it might not seem that way, but for a couple that puts a lot of value into their status, this is probably hell on earth for them. Add in the fact that they are hurting for money, who knows what they would do."

Rae sat down next to Flint once more. "Touché. Well, do you think it's worth talking to them to clear the air? I mean, it couldn't hurt, right? You know chances are that your mom will end up there too, right? You probably should call her first." Rae looked down at her hands before looking back up at Flint.

"Why?"

"'Cause chances are Marie will call your mom and potentially drag her into it anyway. Plus, your mom was very apologetic at the county festival a few weeks ago. Maybe it can help mend broken fences."

"Who knows, but it's worth a shot."

A week later, Flint and Rae were walking up the stairs to

the Hopkins family home. The two held hands as they ascended, and when they reached the top, Rae gently squeezed Flint's hand before letting go. He rang the doorbell and glanced at her once again before his eyes were trained ahead. The seconds felt like minutes before Rae heard the door locks turn. Marie greeted Rae and Flint before she ushered them into her home.

"I'm so glad you both decided to have this meeting. Calvin and Gladys are in the sitting room."

Rae looked around the place and thought it didn't seem like they were suffering from any money woes. Then again, wouldn't a staffer have greeted them at the door if there were still staff around? Shaking her head of all the assumptions swimming through her head, she followed Marie and Flint into the next room.

When they entered, Calvin and Gladys stood up and exchanged greetings before everyone sat down. Rae saw that Marie had left lemonade out for the group.

As if reading her mind, Marie said, "Please take a glass of lemonade." The group stood around awkwardly for a bit before settling down. Gladys spoke up after several seconds of silence.

"Thanks for putting this all together, Marie. How is Cassandra? I haven't seen her in a while."

Marie smiled. "It wasn't a problem. Cassandra is doing well. She's actually out of town right now but should be back next week."

Silence passed through the room once more before Flint cleared his throat. "I'm sure you've probably already heard, but there was a photo of Rae leaked from college."

Calvin coughed briefly, which led to Rae turning her

attention to him. Although she wanted to glare, she kept her composure. Mentally, she told herself to be mature about the situation. "We heard through the grapevine. Do you think we had something to do with it?"

Flint shuffled on the couch until he was leaning forward, arms crossed over his torso. "That would be the question of the day, wouldn't it?"

"Flint—"

"Mom. I'm just asking a question." Rae saw Flint turn his head away from his mom and back to Calvin. "Did you all leak that photo?"

Calvin took a sip of the lemonade in his hand before rubbing his forehead. "No."

His answer took the air out of the room. Rae knew she had worked herself up to the point where she was convinced they had done it, and to have Calvin confirm that they hadn't was a blow. Unless he was lying.

"You didn't leak the photo?" Rae spoke up as she eyed both Marie and Calvin.

"We didn't. There were several photos that our private investigator found, but we leaked none of them. Our objective was to stop you and Flint from being together, not to ruin your career or potentially ruin your life."

The emotions that Rae felt after his comment shook her to a core. "What if not having Flint in my life would have ruined me?"

Silence stretched across the room again before Calvin wiped his forehead. "That wasn't our primary concern. This was essentially a business deal. It's just business."

"That is damn clear," Flint said as he stood up. Rae and Gladys both jumped up with Rae, gently pulling on his arm.

Not knowing exactly what Flint would do or what he was thinking, Rae stood on her tiptoes and whispered in Flint's ear, "He's not worth it." She hoped his comment would make him remember all that he might throw away.

The vein in Flint's neck that pulsed when he got angry was throbbing. Rae's hand moved to grasp Flint's hand in a show of solidarity and support. She watched as Flint's expression lightened, and his breathing slowed down. Rae squeezed his hand before placing her other one on top of his and rubbing the back of his hand with her thumb.

Calvin rubbed the back of his neck before taking a deep breath. "The bottom line is that we have nothing to do with the things that are being thrown in your direction right now. Our lives are already ruined, and we are trying to pick up the pieces as is. Our 'plans' didn't work out the way we thought, so we stopped."

Rae felt Flint tense up at the word *plans*, so she squeezed his hand again to keep him from seeing red. "Do you mind if we take a step outside? Get some fresh air?"

No one had any objections, and Rae led Flint outside to the Hopkins' front porch. They walked down the stairs toward their car just in case there were any cameras around.

"Flint, as shitty as this is to say, you need to get ahold of your emotions. Just because there are no cameras around, that we know of, does not mean that we shouldn't be on. Decking Calvin Hopkins wouldn't be a good look for your campaign, and you and I both know that."

Flint's jaw ticked, and he stuffed his hands in his pockets.

"I know." His words came out as a low growl.

"Look, if I knew this wouldn't end up trending on every

social media site, I wouldn't have stood in your way. But we have a bigger picture to look at here."

Flint didn't have to say anything because Rae could read the dissatisfaction on his face. He glanced down the street, his brooding energy bouncing off of him in spades.

"Let's go."

"Huh?" Rae turned toward him. "You want to leave?" She needed to double-check that she heard him correctly.

"Yep." He unlocked his car and walked Rae over to the passenger side.

"Are you sure? We would be leaving—"

"Yep." The clipped tone and brief answers told Rae that there was no changing his mind about this, so she hopped in the car when he opened the door and waited for him to join her on the driver's side.

Once they were on the road, Rae looked up from her phone and said, "Are you going to at least text your mother and tell her we left?"

Flint nodded. "Do you mind doing it for me?" He took his phone out of his pocket, unlocked it, and handed it to Rae.

"Okay, I just said we had to leave and sorry for the short notice." She handed Flint back his phone, happy to have one crisis averted.

19

———

"Make yourself at home. It feels weird that I'm telling you to make yourself at home in a home that isn't mine, but whatever." Rae chuckled before she closed the door behind Eve. "Flint will come out in a second. Can I get you something to drink? Water? Soda? Hell, wine at this point?"

"Water works." Eve walked over to a chair and sat down before pulling her things out of her bag. When Rae returned, she saw that Eve had set up a makeshift station with her laptop, phone, and pen and paper. As she was placing the glass of water on a coaster, Flint exited his office.

"Hey, Eve, sorry I'm late."

Eve shook her head and said, "You're not late. I'm early." She reached over and grabbed her phone. "I sent you both a list of questions that you both and Flint's campaign have cleared. Everyone was also okay with me tagging along with you guys to a couple of events and campaign activities that might also end up in the article. Are you okay with me recording the conversation?"

The couple nodded.

"Great. And if there is something you don't want included, let me know." The couple nodded again. Eve took a deep breath before announcing, "Let's get started. Flint, why do you want to run for Congress?"

Rae looked on and nodded her head as Flint gave his answers to Eve's questions. The questions ranged from policy questions to a brief mention about Rob Cohen and the campaign he was running. Flint answered them without hesitation but with confidence. Eve took notes in her notebook and a drink of water before looking over at Rae.

"Rae, I'll include biographical information about you and your work at Wild Parks, Wild Lands. There will also be an asterisk next to my name dictating how long we've known each other and our relationship."

"That's great." Rae grinned and readied herself for Eve to ask her questions.

"Let's talk about when you first met."

Rae, with added tidbits from Flint, talked about how they first met, broke up, and then got back together again. She avoided mentioning anything related to the stalking that she had dealt with either time because she didn't want to have to answer questions about it.

"How does it feel to be the significant other of someone running for Congress?"

Rae smiled at the question. "It's exciting. This is something he has wanted to do, and I'm extremely proud of everything he has done so far with the campaign.

They touched on some things they were both passionate about before reaching Eve's last question.

"If given the chance, would you switch places with Flint?"

"What do you mean?" Rae knew that they had cleared this question but hadn't thought of an answer she liked when she was prepping for the interview.

"If you wanted to and had the opportunity, would you run for office, or would you avoid it? If you don't want to include this, that is fine."

Rae looked down at her hands before rolling her shoulders back and looking Eve in her eyes. If this came out wrong, they'd scratch it from the interview, but she was determined to speak from the heart.

"I think it takes a special person to run for Congress. The amount of time, effort, energy, and perseverance that goes into running and being a part of a campaign is mind-blowing. And the strain it puts on the person and the ones they care about most." She felt Flint grasp her hand and give it a small squeeze. "That being said, I understand why Flint wants to do this and how he can carry on the mantle from Rep. John Clarkson. I do my advocacy through my job and helping my community in other ways." Rae ran her fingers through her hair before she caught on that she was doing it and stopped. "That's one of the exceptional things about our nation. There is usually more than one way to do something that can help set the course for improving the world as we know it."

Flint cleared his throat, causing Rae to look at him. "I just wanted to add that I couldn't be doing this without this phenomenal woman next to me. I...haven't been the best at times when it comes to remembering things or having to cancel plans, although I try to keep those few and far between. I know how frustrating that would be for me to have to go through that, and yet Rae is always there. For me and all aspects of my life. There is no way I'll ever be able to repay her for all of this, but I'll spend forever trying." Flint was staring at her now, and she could feel the tears forming in the corners of her eyes.

Eve scribbled some notes down before placing her pen down and looking up. "All right, guys, we're all done here. If you have questions about anything, please let me know. Now, a lot of the questions will probably not make it into the final draft, but I will send you both and the campaign what I come up with."

"This sounds great, Eve. Thanks for taking the time to do this."

"Anytime." With that, Eve packed up her things and left Flint's apartment.

Rae was in the kitchen, drying her hands after she washed the dishes when she heard Flint's phone ring in the living room.

"Flint, your phone is ringing," she yelled as she walked over to the device. She shook her head at him, leaving the phone in the living room and stopped herself from rolling her eyes when she checked to see who was calling. "It's Rick!"

Flint walked back into the room before looking at Rae briefly. "Well, at least he called after Eve finished up the interview, right?"

"True." She handed over the phone.

"What's up, Rick? I was just about to hop back into work since Eve Jackson just finished the interview."

"Actually, could you meet me at the campaign office right now?"

Rae stared at the phone before turning to Flint. Their eyes met, and questions flew between the two of them. Rae knew that Flint's plans included making calls to constituents for the rest of the day, so what was up with the change in plans?

"What happened?"

"It's better if I explain and show it to you in person. I should be at the office in five."

"Sounds good."

Rae hung up the phone for Flint. "What could he be referring to?"

"Your guess is probably about a hundred times better than mine."

20

"What in the entire fuck?"

Flint's words perfectly summed up Rae's thoughts. They had just stepped into the doorway of the campaign office and were surveying the room. The office was a disaster. She imagined that if a tornado had hit Arlington, VA, this was what the destruction might have looked like. Papers were thrown everywhere, tables overturned, chairs tossed to the side. Rick was standing on the other side of the room with his hands on his head. His mouth was agape, and she could see him trying to figure out what to say, but words were not coming out of his mouth.

"We need to call the police. And make sure not to touch anything just in case." Flint's voice was a welcome sound in the silence. It helped break the shock that everyone was feeling. Rick walked over to Flint and started talking to him about the next steps. Rae pulled out her phone and sent a quick text to her friends.

Rae: Flint's campaign office was ransacked. We aren't sure who did it.

She didn't wait for an answer before placing her phone in her back pocket. Rae walked around the wreckage, trying not to disturb any of the items that might lead them to find who broke in and destroyed the office.

She headed to the back of the office, where she found a light shining from the doorway of the woman's bathroom. When she reached the bathroom, she gasped.

"Uh. You guys should probably come over here and see this."

Rick and Flint made their way over to her and followed where her hand was pointed.

In what looked to be red lipstick, someone wrote the word *Revenge* across the mirror.

"I'm not trying to assume, guys, but I think a woman may have destroyed the office."

Rae looked around a bit more before she decided that she needed a change of scenery and went outside to stand on the front steps of the office.

"Rae!"

Rae had been outside for about ten minutes when she looked up and saw Eve a couple of feet away. "What are you doing in Arlington?"

"I had a coffee thing after our interview with someone not too far away, so I figured I would come over to see if I could help in any way."

"You had a date?"

The intrusive voice forced Rae and Eve to snap their heads around to see who was eavesdropping on their conversation.

Kane strolled up to the two women and gave them a lazy smile. He trained his eyes on Eve.

"It wasn't a date. I was trying to get some information for a story I'm working on. Not that I have to explain anything to you."

Rae decided not to tell her she had done just that. At least this time, Eve hadn't been stunned into silence when Kane was in the vicinity. The stare-down between the two drew enough heat that Rae wasn't sure if they wanted to argue or make out in front of her. Either way, she was starting to feel like a third wheel.

"Kane, what are you doing here?"

"Flint told me what happened, and I figured I'd stop by since I was just leaving the Homes for Vets offices."

Rae thought his explanation seemed reasonable, given that the foundation's office was about ten to fifteen minutes away. "Well, follow me. The cops are talking to Flint and Rick inside."

The trio walked into the office, and Kane nodded his head at the women before heading over to where Flint and Rick were talking to the police.

"He drives me nuts."

Rae side-eyed Eve at her comment. "You need to give me the full rundown of what happened between you guys and not just a brief snippet."

"I'll explain it one day."

With that, Rae left it alone. They had more important things to worry about at the moment.

"So," Rae said, trying to change the subject, "do you think you'll still be able to do that profile on Flint? We need to run it by his team, but I'm assuming any press would be a good thing at the moment."

"Should still be fine. I'll run it by Rick when he's done talking to the police. How are things between you and him?"

Rae shrugged. "Not too bad. He hasn't really nitpicked me, but I've also been trying my damnedest to not be the center of attention for any reason other than to help get Flint that congressional seat."

Eve nodded her head. "But I hope you haven't lost yourself in the process."

Rae glanced at her friend before looking at Flint, Rick, Kane, and the police. "What do you mean, lost myself?"

"You've been—how do I say this? So distracted with everything. Not that you don't have a lot going on, but the communication lines haven't been as open as they usually are between us. I'm not speaking for Jules and Liv, by the way. This is just between you and me."

Rae turned her body toward Eve to give her full and undivided attention. She glanced at Eve before looking down at her shoes. "That's not what I meant to do." She then looked up into her friend's eyes. "I apologize if I haven't been as open with everything and not talking with you guys. I've just felt that I'm being pulled in so many directions I'm not sure how to stand up straight anymore."

Eve laid her hand on Rae's shoulder. "And that's why we're here to help. I'm not sure what we can all do, but we do want to be there for you both. Now I'm speaking for Jules and Liv because I know they would say the same thing."

Rae smiled before opening her arms and embracing Eve. The two stayed like that for a moment before they heard an, "Excuse me." When they looked up, more police officers were filing in to examine the crime scene.

"Maybe we should leave?"

"Honestly? That sounds like an awesome plan. Let's go outside, and if the cops need us, they can call us back in." As the two headed toward the front door, Rae looked back and saw that Flint was looking her way. She pointed toward the front door, letting him know she was headed outside, and she and Eve left the office.

"WHEN CAN we get out of here? I'm ready to partake in some of those extracurriculars that you texted me earlier."

The whisper in her left ear made her smile and flipped her brown wavy hair over her right shoulder. She turned her body to face Flint's and stood on her tiptoes to whisper in his ear.

"You wouldn't want your future constituents hearing you say these things."

"I hope they have great sex lives as well. I'm sharing the wealth...but not like that."

That comment made Rae snort and giggle. When she looked up, she saw a smile spread across his face.

"I've missed seeing you smile."

"What do you mean? You see me most days."

"Yes, but you aren't usually smiling. At least not anymore."

Slowly, the smile faded from her face as she realized that he was right. She had stopped smiling as often. Whether it was because of the campaign, work life, etc., or a combination of all the above.

"We should talk about all this later tonight, okay?" Flint glanced up and saw his campaign manager heading over toward him. "Rick is about to interrupt us, but I promise you we will talk tonight, okay?" Rae nodded and accepted his kiss on her cheek. She closed her eyes with a deep sigh before she opened them and turned around to face Rick.

"Hey, Flint, Rae. Outstanding event, am I right?"

Rae nodded and saw Flint do the same out of the corner of her eye.

"Hate to take him away from you, Rae, but he needs to talk to the crowd. I'll bring him right back when he's done."

Rae nodded again, even though she doubted that Flint would be back soon.

"Hey! Sorry, I'm late."

Rae let out a sigh of relief when she turned and saw Eve standing next to her. "Actually, you're right on time. Flint is getting ready to make his speech." She gestured to the podium.

"Great, then I just made it. Glad I was able to swing attending this event since this should be a good component for the profile we're working on." Eve adjusted her purse strap before she said, "How's everything going? Did everything get situated with Flint's office?"

"Kind of." Rae tucked her dark strands behind her ear. "The cops are still investigating the break-in at the office. Staffers and some volunteers came in and helped get everything back in order late last week, so everything is on the up and up again. But I can't help but feel that I'm waiting for the other shoe to drop. Off the record."

That caused Eve to snort, and before either one of them could say another word, Flint stepped up to the microphone. The words that flowed from Flint's lips had his audience sitting on the edge of their seats, focused on Flint's plans for a better future for Arlington. Rae glimpsed just beyond Flint's shoulder and did a double-take. Sarah was standing right over his shoulder, staring back at her. She nudged Eve discreetly, and a few seconds later, Eve whispered, "Is that Sarah? And why is she staring at you?"

"I don't know."

The stare-down turned into a friendly smile and a small wave. The uneasiness that Rae felt about their interaction didn't go away, but she couldn't deal with those feelings right now. She focused her attention back on Flint, who was still giving his speech.

As Flint was reaching the climax of his speech, Rae looked over to the spot where she had seen Sarah previously. But someone else was standing where she once was. Rae searched the crowd to see if she could spot her but couldn't find her again. Goosebumps appeared all over Rae's body. The uneasiness had settled in her stomach. Where had Sarah gone?

"What's wrong?"

Although the event was loud, Eve's question startled her. "Sarah's not there anymore."

"Hm. Maybe she went to the bathroom or went to find a better place to watch Flint's speech?"

"Yeah. Maybe."

The rest of Flint's speech and event went off without a hitch.

"This is probably the fanciest dress I've ever worn." Rae spun around as she examined herself in the full-length mirror.

"And you look stunning in it," Flint said as he walked into the living room while adjusting his bowtie that he couldn't quite get right. Rae looked up from staring at her reflection and turned to face Flint. She walked over to him, not trying to hide the fact that she was checking him out in his tuxedo.

"You don't look too bad yourself."

"Thanks," Flint said as he yanked his bowtie again.

"Here, let me fix it." With ease, Rae retied his bowtie and pressed down on the bow wings, so they lay flat against his neck. "Perfect."

"Yes, you are."

Rae smiled even harder at Flint's compliment before looking down at the navy gown she chose for one of the biggest events she would probably attend this year outside of Flint potentially winning the nomination and the congressional seat. The gown had a small v-cut that showed a hint of cleavage and flowed down to the ground. Thankfully, the heels that Rae choose made it so that the hem of the dress just brushed the ground. The shape of the dress wasn't too tight nor too loose and had a split that went up to her knee, giving her the ability to move with ease. She paired the dress with simple jewelry in order to not draw too much attention to herself.

"Thank you," she whispered. As he was leaning down to kiss her, she swerved her head to the right in order to dodge his kiss. "Sorry, babe. Lipstick is already on."

Flint chuckled. "With those moves, you need to think about becoming a boxer. Your reflexes are pretty good." With that, he kissed her on the forehead and headed to the front closet. He grabbed one of the coats that she had left over at his place and helped her put it on.

"Is the car here?"

"Yes, the driver should be downstairs. Are you ready?"

Rae looked around the apartment once more, trying to take inventory in case she forgot something. She glanced inside the gray clutch and saw that she wasn't missing anything there. "I think I'm ready."

"Excellent. After you," Flint said as he held the door open, and with that, they were on their way to the gala.

With all of the craziness that was going on with preparing for this gala, she hadn't had the opportunity to think about the impact this might have on Flint's chances for winning the congressional seat. D.C. was all about the connections you could make with other people. After all, the city itself was very small, and chances were that if you didn't know some-one, you knew someone who did know that person. Rae wasn't exactly sure who was going to be attending this event, but she wanted to make a good impression nonetheless. Not only for Flint's political chances, but for her career as well.

Those thoughts made her even more nervous. She took several deep breaths and focused on concentrating on the street lights as their driver for the night drove them to their destination.

"How are you doing?"

"You know, it's funny and scary how easily you're able to tell when something is wrong or if I'm feeling some type of way."

"Nice attempt at changing the subject. Are you okay?"

Rae rolled her eyes but appreciated Flint's honesty. "Yeah, I'm just nervous about tonight."

"Everything is going to be fine. Plus, Jules is attending this event, so you have someone else to talk to."

"That's true. I don't want to stop her from doing her job, however. And who's to say your parents won't show up."

"Good point. And I know they have tickets for it, but not sure if they'll be able to make it due to some work obligations my dad mentioned yesterday. For the most part, this might end up with me dragging you from person to person, introducing you to people, etc. There will be a lot of handshaking."

"And that's why I put hand sanitizer in my clutch. I'm not going to bust it out after every handshake, but I have a sneaky suspicion that it will be put to good use. You also can't go wrong with a good hand cream after the fact."

"That works, babe."

Rae turned to look at Flint and noticed that his leg was bouncing up and down.

"Are you nervous?"

"Yeah, and I don't know why."

"Well, it's probably the biggest moment of your life outside of when you get elected to that seat."

Flint smirked at her reply. "I'm glad you have faith in my electability, but the biggest moment of my life was when you walked back into it."

Rae opened her mouth a couple of times to reply, but nothing left her lips. A grin appeared on her lips before she said, "I'd have to agree with that."

Flint gave her a quick peck on the lips before he asked, "Did I get any on me?"

"No, but it would serve you right if you did. I warned you about the lipstick." Although she tried to sound stern, her laughter gave her away.

"It was worth the risk." Flint grabbed her hand and gently squeezed it before looking out the window.

A few moments later, Rae spoke. "Is there anything I can do to help you ease your nerves?"

"I know several things we could do, but all of them probably shouldn't happen in the back seat of a town car."

Rae rolled her eyes and chuckled at Flint before he continued, "Just having you here is helping to them."

"I'm glad." They continued their small talk until they arrived at the venue. When Rae exited the car with Flint on her arm, she looked up in amazement. "Are we really going in there?"

"That's the plan." With that, he led Rae up the stairs and into the National Building Museum. Rae had been in the museum before, but she had never seen it transformed quite like this. The main floor had been separated into two different event spaces. One area had tabletops where people could enjoy drinks and hors d'oeuvres. She assumed the curtain that was dividing the room was where they would be having dinner and seeing presentations. At least Flint told her they would be having dinner here, and if he was mistaken, she would need to grab some fast food within the hour. Just as Rae had gotten some snacks in her belly and she and Flint were quietly chatting amongst themselves at one of the tabletops, she saw something out of the corner of her eye. Before she could register what it was, Flint whispered. "Rob Cohen is making his way towards us."

She kept her sigh to herself as she took a drink from her wine glass and plastered a smile on her face. She then turned around to face the person that she knew was going to cause trouble.

"West, Rachelle. It's great to see you here tonight."

"It's Flint, and although I don't need to speak for her, she goes by Rae."

"Ah, I knew that. I apologize." Rae nodded in acknowledgment of his apology but did nothing else. She was happy he didn't extend his hand for a handshake because she didn't want to touch him but also didn't want to come across as being impolite. "I just wanted to come over and say how sorry I am about what happened to your campaign office. Whoever did it was completely out of line, and that type of behavior shouldn't be allowed in politics."

"I appreciate your kind words."

"Anyway, the reason I came over here was to make sure that you knew that I'm hoping whoever did this is brought to justice quickly. We can't have this tainting the hard work that we both are putting into all of this."

"Can I take your picture?"

The conversation was interrupted by someone holding a camera. Rae assumed they were a staffer as the three got together and smiled for the camera. The camera's flash went off several times before the staffer gave them a thumbs up when he was done taking the photos. With that, both Rob and the staffer were on their way.

"He's involved." Rae finished the rest of her drink before placing her glass down on the cloth-covered table.

"You got that feeling too?"

Rae nodded. "I think it's more than a feeling."

"Why?"

"Outside of the fact that he didn't sound sorry at all for what happened to your campaign office and the fact that I don't think it was a coincidence that he came over just as that staffer was taking photos? He knew my name was Rachelle. That isn't well known, so someone has been doing their homework on us."

22

Another day, another evening that Rae was spending the night at Flint's house. They were enjoying a television show that Rae had found while flipping through the channels when Rae jumped off the couch.

"Is everything okay?" Flint looked at his girlfriend, examining her with concern.

"Yes! I just forgot something." She jogged over to her purse that she had left on the dining room table. She dug through it, trying to find the item she wanted, and once she did, she wrapped her fist around it. "I have a surprise for you."

Rae turned around and tried to contain the smile that was threatening to come from her lips. She walked back over to the couch, where Flint had since stood up, and placed her closed fists out in front of her. "I want you to pick a hand."

Flint raised an eyebrow at her but didn't question what she was doing. He smirked when he picked her left hand, and when she turned it over and opened her fist, there was nothing there. He said, "Darn," and dramatically snapped his fingers. "There was only a fifty percent chance of me guessing wrong, and I still managed to do so."

Rae chuckled before pulling her hand back. She then held out her right fist for Flint. "So, you know whatever I'm holding is in my right hand. Any guesses?"

"You could be tricking me and have nothing in either hand."

Rae playfully rolled her eyes and said, "I promise there is something in my right hand. Want to guess what it could be?"

Flint thought for a moment before shaking his head. "I have no idea besides the fact that it must be something tiny."

"Oh, you're no fun." Rae stuck her tongue out at Flint before opening her fist. In the palm of her hand was a key. "This is to my apartment."

Flint stared at her with his mouth slightly agape. It took him a moment to catch on, but when he did, he grabbed her into a bear hug, lifting her off the ground.

"I guess this was an excellent surprise?"

"One of the best." He finished his comment with a kiss on her lips.

The ringing of a phone startled Rae out of her sleep. Just as quickly as the ringing started, it stopped, and Rae promptly fell back to sleep. Or so she thought.

Rae's eyes sprung open as she looked around the room. Memories of the evening before swam back into her consciousness, and a smile appeared on her face. She turned over and reached for Flint, but he wasn't there. Assuming that he must be somewhere else in the apartment, she leaned over to grab her purse from the night before. Rae found her phone quickly and checked the time. Realizing that she slept in later than she intended to, she climbed out of the bed and dashed into the bathroom. Once she finished washing off the rest of the makeup she'd missed the night before and brushing her teeth, Rae headed back into the bedroom and grabbed a sweatshirt she had stolen from Flint two months ago. She headed out into the living room, where she saw Flint hunched over his laptop, vigorously typing.

"Is everything all right?" Rae asked as she glanced over at Flint before continuing on her way to the kitchen.

"I'm not sure."

Rae stopped in her tracks and turned around. "What's up? Or should I get the cup of coffee first?"

Flint glanced up at her before looking back at his laptop. "You'd probably want to get wine given how this day is going."

Rae checked the time on the microwave before reaching to open the cabinet with mugs in it. "Coffee will probably have to do since it's too early for wine." She stopped in her tracks with her hand on the doorknob. "I never thought I would say that," she mumbled to herself. Rae dashed around his kitchen to finish making her coffee before settling down next to Flint on his couch.

"So, what did you need to tell me that I should probably have grabbed a glass of wine for?"

Flint stopped typing and placed the laptop on the coffee table in front of him. "There is something I haven't told you."

Rae braced herself for what might be coming. She took a sip from her coffee and placed it down on a coaster. When Flint didn't continue, she motioned with her hands for him to keep going.

"You know how we reconnected at your job?"

Rae's eyes had drifted to her hands before flying back up to Flint's face. "Yes." She did her best not to show any emotion while she studied the man in front of her.

"That wasn't a coincidence."

"This isn't the first time I've heard this." Memories from her conversation with her mom came flowing back. She had forgotten to ask him about it with everything else going on.

Flint, who had been staring at the wall in front of him, whipped his head around to look at Rae. "Who told you that?"

"My mom insinuated that everything wasn't a coincidence and brought up the fact that you talked to Jules about me, but I think that's all she knew. Anyway, continue."

Flint rubbed his hands over his face before placing them on his thighs as he let out a deep sigh. The longer he took to respond, the more Rae's stomach jumped. Rae could feel her breath quickening as she tried to calm her nerves down. Would he just spit it out?

Rae cleared her throat, and that brought Flint's eyes back to hers.

"It wasn't a coincidence. I—I knew you were being hired, and a few months later, I volunteered to take on that case once I knew that you would be the person I would work with directly."

Rae's face remained blank as she processed the news. She massaged her temples and then loosened her ponytail to relieve the tension. A headache was forming, and she was taking some precautionary measures to help prevent it from getting worse.

"I'm pissed you didn't tell me this, but okay. Is that it?"

Flint shook his head. "Not by a long shot. Kane found out

that the leaker is going to announce that I am the reason that you got your job."

"Excuse me?" Rae stared Flint down as she stood up from her seat. She put her hand out to tell him that she didn't want him to speak before she grabbed her coffee. Rae turned her back on him when she walked over to the window as she felt the anger rising in the back of her throat. *One. Two. Three. Four. Five. Six. Seven. Eight. Nine. Ten.* She took another deep breath before turning around to face Flint.

"You didn't have any say in getting me hired, right? Like you didn't 'put in a good word for me'?"

Flint slowly shook his head. "I only knew that you were working there after you had started your first day. Someone on my team brought up your name in passing, and I did a little research to make sure it was you, including confirming with Jules. I thought it might be a way for us to talk again."

Rae let out a breath that she hadn't even realized she had been holding. Although she was upset Flint hadn't told her this from the get-go, at least he wasn't the reason she got hired for the job.

"I'm still pissed at you for only just telling me this now, but we have bigger issues to deal with. What can we do to stop this made-up fairy tale that this person or people are spinning?"

23

The leaker was true to their word, and gossip was published about how Rae had gained her employment. Rae proactively told Danielle, her boss, who took the news up the chain of command. Danielle told her not to worry about it and that Wild Parks, Wild Lands would make a statement, confirming the conditions of Rae's employment. Rae also gave another quote stating that it was preposterous that she would have gotten a job because of someone that she hadn't been in contact with for years, and that she had worked hard to get this job and to get where she was in her career.

A few days later, Rae was in her office working on talking points for a policy when she heard a knock on the door.

"Come in."

She wasn't surprised to see Danielle on the other side of the door. Danielle gave Rae a slight smile that wavered before it disappeared completely. This made the hairs on Rae's neck stand up at attention.

"What's up?" Rae asked as she watched Danielle grab one

of the seats in front of her desk. Danielle's mouth opened to say something, but nothing came out. Was she getting fired?

"There is something I wanted to discuss with you." Yep, she was getting fired.

"What's going on?"

"There has been a lot of attention surrounding you, Flint, and his campaign."

"Yes, I know it isn't ideal, and I apologize for all the attention that has now been thrown at Wild Parks, Wild Lands. That wasn't my intention."

"Of course not. Who would want to have photos leaked of them? I had some wild moments in college myself, and I'm thankful that a) there is no photographic evidence, and b) that social media wasn't a thing when I was there. And we know you had nothing to do with this latest news about whether Flint was involved with you getting your job here." Danielle's brief grin made Rae assume that she was thinking about some of those wild times in college. "That being said, everyone supports you here, and you aren't going to lose your job."

Rae let out the breath that she hadn't realized she was holding in. Couldn't she have started this conversation with that? "Whew. Okay, that's great because I love working here."

Danielle took a deep breath before blowing it out. "That being said, would you be okay with working from home for the time being?"

Rae stared at Danielle, processing the news. "Does that include me not going to Capitol Hill?"

Danielle nodded. "This wasn't my decision, but some of our funders are worried that it could be a distraction in meetings with congressional members and their staffers."

Rae looked away as she tried to stop the tears that were threatening to fall from her eyes. She had worked so hard to get to where she was, and now she was being limited because of someone having it out for her. "I understand."

"I'm so sorry. If you have any questions or need anything from me, please let me know."

Rae nodded, and when she looked up into Danielle's eyes, she saw that her eyes were watering. Saving them both from having a crying session together, Danielle left the room, closing the door behind her. Only then did Rae let the tears fall.

When Rae got home that evening, she put the stuff that she could carry home from the office down on her dining room table before she headed into her bedroom to change into something more comfortable. She hadn't told anyone about what had happened today because she wasn't sure what to say. Once she felt a tad bit more relaxed in her sweats, she began unpacking to set up a makeshift office in her dining room. Her progress was interrupted when her phone buzzed from its spot on the table. She paused and checked the notification. It was from Flint.

Flint: Hey babe, hadn't heard from you in a while. Are you doing okay?

Part of her wanted to ignore his message and just continue doing what she was doing. The other part told her that shutting down wouldn't do her any good, and talking to someone might help her process her feelings. Plus, she would eventually have to tell him anyway, so was there a point in hiding it now?

She flipped the phone over and over in her hands, debating what she should do. Rae placed the phone back on the dining room table and went back to unpacking her things from the office.

"Where is it?" she mumbled as she looked through her purse. Her laptop charger was nowhere to be found.

"Son of a—" She stopped herself before the curse words flew out of her mouth. She checked her phone once again and saw that it was 7:37 p.m. She had her badge that would allow her to get into the office after hours, but she didn't even want to think about having to travel back to work right now. Rae glanced up at her window and noted how dark it was outside. She could stop by in the morning and grab the charger before heading back home, but that was a lot of work, especially when she could just do it right now. Although her job wasn't too far from her apartment, she figured driving there might be easier and quicker, given the time of day. She double-checked that she had her office badge and grabbed her purse, coat, and baseball cap before she headed out to her car.

Once Rae was settled in her car, she debated calling Flint to keep her company on the drive over to her office. After tossing the idea around in her head for a couple of seconds, she figured what harm would it do and called him.

"Hey, babe." She'd never tire of him calling her that.

"Hey, yourself. I saw your text message and thought it was easier to call you back."

"Makes sense. I was just checking in to see how you were doing."

Rae sighed before replying. "To be honest, I'm not doing too hot. I'm on my way back to my office now."

"What happened?" She could hear his fingers flying across a keyboard in the background.

"I kind of got demoted."

Flint said nothing, but the typing in the background stopped. "What? Why?"

"Because of the picture thing. I guess it was bringing too much unwanted attention to the organization. I'm guessing I'm lucky they didn't fire me." One stray tear fell down her cheek.

"You've got to be shitting me." Rae could hear the anger in Flint's voice.

"Nope. But I get it. They are, after all, an organization that is trying to help the environment. I wouldn't want anyone who is a part of the public face of my organization bringing unwarranted attention either. It makes sense, even though it's crappy for me. Like I said, I'm surprised they didn't just fire me."

Flint took a deep breath, and she assumed he was trying to calm down his anger. "Is there anything I can do to help?"

"Would you be able to come over tonight? I haven't checked your schedule, so I'm sorry if it's blocked off." She wiped another tear from her face. She needed to focus more on driving and less on crying, even though she couldn't stop the tears from flowing. Rae thought she could keep it together, but that was a mistake. She thanked herself for grabbing the baseball cap that she hoped would cover her face in case anyone was still around the office when she arrived.

"I'm supposed to have a couple of appearances tonight. One I have to attend, or it will look bad, but the other I could probably send someone in my place. I was actually just wrapping up to head to the first event now."

Just like that, Rae felt guilty. Flint had events he needed to attend for his campaign, and here she was burdening him with her problems. "You know what, don't worry about it. You already said you would attend these events, and I don't want you to cancel because of me."

"But you need me."

Rae choked back a sob to keep up the wall she was building. "I know, but it can wait until after you're done. I can call my mom or the girls or something."

"Only if you're sure. I have no problem leaving early."

"It's fine. I'm at my office, so I should probably go."

"Okay. Let me know when you get home, and if you need me to come home early, I will."

"Will do." Rae pulled into a parking spot down the block from her office and put her car in park.

"I love you."

"I love you too," she whispered before she hung up the phone. She grabbed her purse, stepped out of the car, and locked the door before she walked down the street to her office building.

A few minutes later, Rae was kneeling on the floor of her office. She had just finished looking under her desk for her charger, but it was nowhere to be found. *Where the hell is it?* She tore open her drawers and rifled through the contents in them, but still nothing. After spending twenty minutes looking around every place she could think of, including a couple of conference rooms that she usually frequented, she threw her hands up in the air and gave up. The charger was gone. Figuring that she would just contact the tech team or order an extra one herself when she got home, she grabbed the rest of her things and headed back to her car.

The ride back to her apartment was uneventful. She was

in the middle of texting Flint to let him know that she had arrived home safely when she kicked something on the floor. She looked down at the object and gasped. There on her welcome mat was her charger and an envelope.

Rae dropped her phone into her purse and picked up the items in front of her. Maybe her charger fell out of her purse when she was on her way home, and someone found it and placed it in front of her door. She juggled holding the items in her arms with opening the door, but she made it to the dining room table without dropping anything.

"Why would someone include an envelope with my charger?" she mumbled as she opened the envelope. There was a terse note inside.

Rae,

To prevent more things from being leaked, Flint must drop out of the race. There's plenty more from where those pictures came from.

Rae's blood turned cold.

24

———

Silence. That is the sound that greeted Rae as she shut her bathroom door. Rae turned the faucet on and stared as the water flooded into the tub. After watching the water for a few seconds, she walked over to a basket she kept in the corner of her bathroom, picked out a bath bomb that she hadn't tried, and placed it in the tub. Turning to the counter, she grabbed a makeup wipe and removed the products she had placed on her face. Rae stared at herself as she wiped away the makeup she had worn that day. The small bags under her eyes became more noticeable under the bathroom lights. Distracting herself with other thoughts to avoid staring at her face further, she made her way back over to the bathtub and took off the clothes she had worn when she went back to her office. She then slipped into the tub. As every inch of her body met the warm, bubbly water, she felt herself relax. Rae didn't bother tying her hair up to avoid getting it wet because she knew that she was way past caring about her hair at this point.

These last few months had been chaotic, and what did

she have to show for it? She was, she thought, the perfect significant other to someone who was running for office. Yet here she was, sitting in this tub, thinking about her choices. All of this was based on how other people thought of her. Although she didn't want what other people thought of her to get to her, she was having a hard time letting them roll off her shoulders.

Rae sucked in a deep breath and let it out slowly. What the hell was she going to do?

She sunk deeper into the tub, covering even more of her body with the warm waves and bubbles. Rae leaned her head until it rested on the wall behind her. Still, the only sound she heard was the waves in her bath, forming around her moving body, although she had forgotten to bring the new candles she had gotten a few days ago with her into the bathroom.

She was tired of all the bullshit. Having to be extra proper for the campaign, yet getting beat up on the sidelines while pretending to be something she wasn't. All of Rick's thoughts and suggestions weren't painful per se, but she didn't like feeling that she would never be good enough. This didn't even touch on what happened to her because someone didn't want Flint running for office. Nor did it factor in the strain that it was having on her and Flint's relationship. Did it?

"Rae."

The sound of her name almost made her jump out of her skin. The bubbles and water sloshed around, causing some of them to spill onto the floor.

Rae's hand flew to her chest. "What did I say about you sneaking up on me?"

"I thought you saw me this time. It's kind of hard to hide when I knocked on the door and opened it, although you seemed to be lost in your own world. I'll clean that up." Flint took off his already undone tie and his suit jacket. He grabbed one of the towels that were on the towel rack and wiped up the mess that had been made.

"I was. In my own little world, that is."

"Anything you want to talk about?"

"There's a lot I want to talk about, but first, what are you doing here? I thought you had events to go to tonight?"

"I sent Rick and Kate. You're going through a lot, and you're more important."

Rae's words were stuck in her throat as she processed what he had just said. "But this is your dream."

"You're my dream. None of this means anything without you. None. Of. It." He leaned over to kiss her three times, emphasizing each word.

"Funny you should mention that. I received a note today that said you had to drop out in order for all of this to stop."

"I saw it on your dining room table when I walked in. Is that what you want me to do?"

Rae thought about it for a moment before putting her head in her hands. She took a deep breath before showing her face again. "It would make things a lot easier on me. I wouldn't have Rick bugging me about the clothes I wear, and these threats would supposedly stop." She turned her head toward Flint. "We'd also get to see each other more."

"True. Is this what we want to do?"

Rae and Flint watched each other momentarily before Rae broke the silence. "Do you want to join me in here? I think this tub could fit both of us." She knew that Flint had to notice that she changed the subject, but he said nothing. He stripped the clothes he had worn to work from his body and stepped into the tub behind Rae. The two took their time getting settled, hoping to avoid putting more puddles on Rae's bathroom floor.

Flint got to work on massaging Rae's shoulders, which was something she didn't even know she had wanted. He worked out one kink in her neck that almost had her moaning. "So, you asked what I thought we should do about the campaign?"

"Hmm," Flint murmured as he continued working his magic on her shoulders.

"Part of me wants to say *screw this* and take off for the hills, but I'm not a quitter." She looked over her shoulder into Flint's eyes, causing him to stop his movements. "We'll finish this race together whether you win or lose. Deal?"

"Deal."

Rae turned her head back around and sighed in contentment. She moved further down into the water and said, "We just need to figure out what to do next about this person or people who don't want to see you make it to the finish line."

25

The next day, Rae was in the middle of doing an at-home barre class to keep herself busy. She figured it was a good way to burn off some excess energy she had after the day was done. Although it was only a day into her working from home routine, she was pretty much over it. She thrived on talking to people, and since Flint wasn't there to keep her company, she could only be with her thoughts. Which was troubling to her.

The more she thought about everything going on, the more it saddened her that it had come to this.

About halfway through the video, her phone buzzed. She ignored it at first, figuring if it was important, someone would have called her and not sent a text message. But then her phone buzzed again. And then again.

"Why didn't I just silence the damn thing?" muttered Rae as she walked over to her coffee table where she placed the remote and her phone. She paused the barre video and checked her notifications. Rae was expecting a text versus a notification from the camera she had set up outside of her apartment door. The hairs on Rae's neck stood up before she calmed herself down. As she was looking for the camera's app in her phone, her phone started ringing, causing her to almost drop it.

"Hey, Jules," she whispered. She grabbed a sweater she hung over the side of her couch days ago.

"Hey!" Jules paused for a moment. "Why are you whispering?"

"Jules, I think someone's at my door. I was just about to check my camera's video feed when you called."

"Oh, shit." It was rare that Jules cursed. "Do you want me to call the police?"

Rae shook her head, although she couldn't be seen. "Not right this second, but if you don't hear from me in ten minutes, could you call the police and then my parents and Flint? Just in case?" Rae hated that she had to even think like this, but it was better to be safe than sorry.

"Sounds good. Be careful." With that, Jules hung up. Rae quickly pulled up the live feed to see if anyone was still out there, and she saw what she assumed was an ominous shadow's head bopping up and down into and out of frame. Having had enough of this, she walked over to the hallway and grabbed the bat she kept there from when Flint scared her half to death when he arrived at her apartment late one night a few weeks ago. She also set her phone to record, just in case it could be used as evidence should something happen to her. Placing the phone in a small pocket of her exercise pants, she took a deep breath as she walked down the hallway to her front door. She quietly unlocked the door and pulled it open with all her might, drawing back the bat over her head in one fluid motion.

"Who are you and what the fuck are you doing outside my house?!" Her voice portrayed more courage than she was feeling as she stood there, slightly shaking while holding the bat.

The figure who had on a dark-colored hoodie and pants jumped before they stopped moving.

"Turn around slowly and drop whatever you might be holding."

"I'm not holding anything."

The voice took Rae's breath away, and as she stared at the person, they slowly turned around.

"Sarah?" she asked. "What are you doing here? How do you know where I live?"

Sarah, who had been staring at the ground, moved toward Rae with her hands up. Rae lowered the bat slightly when Sarah came into the small rays of light that were emitting from Rae's front porch and a nearby street lamp.

"I want to talk to you about some things that have been going on with Flint's campaign. Could we talk about this inside?"

Rae was a little wary about letting Sarah into her apartment because she had never told her the location.

"You must be outside your mind if you think I'll let you into my house after I found you creeping outside of my window. We can talk out here." Rae clutched her cell phone tighter. She didn't like where this was going. "Explain yourself."

"I was coming here to spy on you. And I—uh—leaked your college photo to the press and on social media."

Rae did a double-take. That came out easier than expected, but she also doubted that she heard that correctly. "You leaked the photo?"

Sarah nodded, further confirming Rae's worst fears.

"Why would you do this?"

Sarah blinked but said nothing. Rae's stare was forced into a glare as she waited for a response. "Well, are we just going to stand here and stare at one another?"

Sarah shook her head and looked down before she ran her fingers through her hair.

"Who are you working for?"

Sarah hesitated. Rae could see the wheels in her head turning.

"Don't get all shy now. You came all the way over here to talk, so talk." Rae could feel her anger rising. She adjusted the sweater she had put on when she stopped her workout, pulling it tighter across her body. Although it was warming up, there was still a chill in the air.

"I did this because I needed the money. They offered me a job that required me to find out more information on you. It came out of nowhere, but everything checked out with the company I was working for."

"Who are they? Who are you working for? Wait a minute, hold that thought." Rae loosened her grip on her phone and unlocked it. She flipped through her apps, found the one she wanted, and clicked on it. When the app loaded, she pressed the red button on the screen. "I would like for you to repeat everything that you said and continue to have this conversation recorded. Are you okay with that? This is also you giving consent to being recorded."

Sarah nodded her head and said, "It doesn't matter anyway, I'm screwed." She then repeated the information that she gave to Rae. "I work for Edwards, Holland, and Walker Consulting, which is otherwise known as EHWC. One of their tasks to help their clients is to dig up information on other people."

"Kind of like a private investigator?"

"Sort of. I was offered a job because I lived with you a few years ago, and they figured that I must've had some dirt on you that could hurt Flint's campaign."

"Did they ever tell you who, at the company, wanted the information that you would provide?"

Sarah licked her lips and looked Rae in her eyes. "No. I was just told the information would be super important for a congressional race in the D.C. area and that they would pay for my room and board, a salary, and all of my other expenses that I accrued when I was on the job while I was out here. Then they mentioned your name and that you were dating Flint. I didn't know you were back in contact with him, let alone dating him."

"That's beside the point. So, this job is what brought you back to Washington, D.C."

Sarah nodded again. "Yes. I went back to my hometown after I got laid off from my job. I couldn't find much there and worked several jobs at once to try to help my family out at home. Then I had the opportunity to come back here, plus a job that offered me more money than I'd ever seen, so I took the leap." Rae could see the tears welling up in her eyes.

"Did you have anything to do with the ransacking of Flint's campaign office?"

It was Sarah's turn to do a double-take as her eyes widened in shock.

"I have no idea what you're talking about, and whatever that is, I had nothing to do with it. My only task was to see if I could find more information about you and dig up some embarrassing photos that could be leaked to the media. I was just supposed to send whatever I had to this email address, and that was it."

Sarah sniffled before she continued. "And it was at your expense. I'm so sorry. I was desperate, but I still shouldn't have done it. I'm probably causing an even bigger mess for myself because I signed an NDA." With that declaration, the tears flowed down Sarah's face.

Although Rae was angry, she still felt guilty based on what Sarah told her. She stopped recording and closed her front door, and gestured for Sarah to follow her. Rae sat down on the steps in front of her apartment, and Sarah sat down a few inches away on the same step. Rae debated comforting her but decided against it. She waited for Sarah to somewhat pull herself together.

"You know," Sarah said as she took a deep breath to calm her tears, "I didn't expect you to be so nice when I spilled my guts to you. I figured this day was coming, eventually."

"I just know that me getting even more angry about this won't solve anything. Plus, you might be the key that helps unravel this entire scheme. And I appreciate the fact that you were more forthcoming with information than I expected."

"I'm not sure how else I can help. I told you all that I know."

"But there might be something else there. We have to figure out who wanted your services." Rae thought for a moment before she said, "I'll start recording again if you don't mind."

Sarah nodded her head and brushed her hair off of her shoulders. Rae angled her phone so that it caught Sarah's face and testimony, although it was evening, and the lighting wasn't the greatest.

"Did you receive any file or information about me? How did they communicate with you?"

"Yes, I received a file on you. Well, kind of. It gave the basics like where you live, hence how I'm here now." Sarah pointed at Rae's front door. "It was a decent overview of all the things you've done over the years, and it was my job to fill in the gaps."

"And nothing in that document gave any hint to who might have hired you?"

"Not that I can think of. I don't have the document because my bosses didn't want to leave a paper trail." Sarah's eyes darted upward, and Rae paused her questioning. "Wait."

Rae watched as Sarah mouthed some words to herself. Was she trying to recall something from the file they gave her?

"It wasn't in the file. It was something I was told by one of the men who hired me. He mentioned the bigger splash it could play on social media, the better. They were trying to affect the political race."

That comment sent the wheels in Rae's head turning. Leaking "embarrassing" photos of her wouldn't do much damage to her reputation because she could have just ignored it. Who would it damage?

"Flint," she whispered as the realization hit. She wasn't the target of this latest stalking. They were going after Flint.

"Shit. We've been looking at this all wrong," Rae mumbled to herself.

"What was that?"

Rae had almost forgotten that Sarah was there. "Uh, nothing. Let's wrap this up. But don't go anywhere. I assume everyone will want to talk to you too."

26

Rae held her breath as she waited for Flint to flip the light switch. When the light radiated throughout the room, Rae's breath turned into a sigh of relief. The campaign headquarters was back to looking the way it had before the destruction. Rae knew that the campaign staffers had worked overtime to make sure that the office was back up and running, but she didn't know what to expect when they entered. It had already been enough chaos dealing with the media over the break-in and journalists making the connection between this and her leaked college photo.

She glanced around at her friends, so happy that they could take time out of their schedules to join Flint as they tried to figure out who was responsible for this. Because this needed to end now.

"Is Kane coming? Should we wait for him?" Rae took a quick glance at Eve to see if she reacted to his name but saw her eyes shift slightly before returning Rae's gaze. She raised an eyebrow, almost daring her to utter a word. Rae gave Eve a knowing smile before getting down to business.

"Whoever this person or people are, they have brought enough pain and dysfunction, and I refuse to live like this anymore." Rae was pacing back and forth as her three best friends and her boyfriend watched her like a tennis match. Rick was on Flint's cell phone and chimed in when necessary. "I think we need to go talk to Rob."

Jules and Liv shared a look between one another as Rick spoke up on the phone. "I already talked to Rob's team, and they claimed they had nothing to do with this."

"Oh, come on. Who would freely admit to trying to do something underhanded to sabotage a campaign?" Rae had had enough.

"She's right. And he stands the most to gain if I drop out."

Rae's and Flint's eyes met, and she felt her heart rate calm down as she looked into his crystal-clear blue eyes. He was the calming force that usually kept her sane.

"Does anyone have any ideas about how we can corner him? I mean, ask him questions?"

Rae couldn't stop the laughter that fell from her lips at Liv's comment and the cough she tried to use to cover her snafu. "Good questions."

A knock on the door quieted the giggles. Flint was sitting closest to the door, so he got up and answered it. In walked Kane, who waved to the room as he walked over to grab another dining room chair so he could sit down. Rae watched as he looked around the room, and his eyes settled on Eve before he turned his attention back to Rae. "Sorry for being late."

"You're just on time. We were talking about Rob having

the most to gain if Flint left the campaign, so we were wondering if he hired EHWC to dig up information on us to force Flint out of the race. After all, Sarah was told to find things that would cause a big splash." Rae was glad that she told Sarah that she could leave instead of having her meet with the rest of the group. She didn't trust her, and if they were talking about plans, she didn't want her to leak them to the people she was working for.

"Um." Rae paced a few lengths as the group sat in silence, following her moves as she tried to come up with a way to talk to Rob.

"Rick, as we're winding down before the primaries, are there any more events that you know of that Rob might attend as well? Maybe we can pull him to the side and question him there?"

Rae was thankful that Flint thought of that suggestion.

"There is a fundraiser just before the primary. But it's at least a month away, I think. I'll need to check with Mallory, who handles our scheduling, to make sure. There might be a couple of meet-and-greets coming up, but let me dig up Flint's schedule."

Flint swore, and Rae slid her hands down her face.

"Wait. Why are you guys talking about waiting for a fundraiser that's a month away? Isn't there a good excuse that we can use to see him sooner?" Jules had a point.

"I mean, I could accidentally trip him on the street. I can act like I was attending an event he was doing and walk up to him with a sign and completely fangirl out and—"

"You really thought this through, huh?" Rae said before she chuckled at Liv's comment. Liv shrugged in response.

"Would it be silly to have Jules call and ask for an

appointment with Cohen's office? Wait. That might not work because I assume his team, even if they didn't hire the private investigators, would have probably found out that we were great friends."

"And Homes for Vets would be out because of Flint's connection to it." It was the first time Eve had spoken in a while, and Rae watched as Eve's eyes were focused on her versus looking at Kane, whose eyes weren't wavering from her.

"Not necessarily." All eyes swung to Kane as he smiled at Flint with his arms folded over his chest. Flint stared at him for a second before returning the smile.

"We missed something, didn't we?"

Rae looked at Flint, then at Kane, and then back at Flint. "I think we did, Liv."

"What are you guys thinking about?"

"So, technically, Home for Vets hasn't officially endorsed anyone." Rae watched as everyone who didn't know that fact swung around and looked at Kane.

"But wouldn't everyone assume that you would endorse and campaign to support the cofounder of the foundation?"

"Not if they're joining other veteran organizations in the area to host a meet-and-greet."

"He's right." Rick's voice pierced through Flint's phone. "A bunch of veteran organizations are hosting a meet the candidates event about a week and a half from now. Rob would be silly not to go because this would be an enormous opportunity to get support from the military and veterans. He could try to swipe some support from Flint, too, who is the only veteran running in the primary."

A light bulb went off in Rae's head. "Kane, since Home for

Vets is a sponsor of this event, would you happen to have the attendance list? When I plan events for Wild Parks, Wild Lands, I keep track of who's coming. It only makes sense to."

"Right, 'cause you need to order food and beverages, etc. for the event. I'm also willing to bet the guest list, including the press, is pretty much set right now because it's only about a week out."

The mention of the press caused Eve to stare at Liv. "I wonder if I might be able to get an invitation to this event as well? Maybe pull a few strings to see if I can wrangle a press pass."

"Don't worry. If you can't, I can add you as my guest. Free of charge."

Rae let the smirk she was fighting fly free on her face as she watched to see Eve's reaction to Kane's words. *Let's see Eve talk her way out of this one.*

"I'd probably have no issue trying to get one. Thanks, though."

"Are you sure? Even Liv said the guest list might be closed at this point."

"I'm. Sure."

"Well then," Rae said, directing the attention back to her. Eve was about ready to bare her teeth, so it was time to jump in. "Kane, do you have access to the list?" Rae looked back at Kane and saw that he was busy on his phone.

"Here it is," Kane said as he handed his phone over to Rae. Her hands slightly shook when she took it from his grasp.

Rae held her breath as she scanned the list before a smile appeared on her face.

"He's scheduled to be there. And he's bringing a guest."

27

"Is your stomach in your throat too? Or maybe it's just me." Although Rae was talking to Flint, her eyes never moved from the passenger side window, watching the buildings change into trees the farther away they got from the city. Rae felt the slight tension in the car as they traveled to the meet-and-greet. She didn't want that gloomy cloud following them in addition to whatever might unravel at the event.

"I'm a little nervous too." Rae glanced over at Flint when he didn't elaborate. His clutched hands on the steering wheel told her he was more than just a little nervous.

"The worst that could happen is that we cause a scene and end up on the front page of the *Washington Post*."

"That's the worst thing that could happen."

Rae smoothed out the long pink and white sundress that she had worn that day. "Listen, I don't know about you, but I'm pretty used to having my name smeared on the internet so I think front-page news would be a step up."

Rae watched as Flint tried to stop his lips from twitching

but failed. A hearty laugh left his mouth, dissolving some tension in the car.

"When we get there, I need to go to the bathroom as soon as possible." Rae wiggled in her seat, trying to control her bladder.

"I told you should have slowed down on chugging that water that you had to have just before we left."

Rae rolled her eyes. "It wasn't my fault. I was thirsty, but I can hold it until we get there."

Soon, the couple pulled up to a country club and got out of the car. Rae took several deep breaths as an employee took them back to the banquet room where the event would occur. As they were gathering their name badges, Rae scanned the remaining badges to see if she could find Rob's but didn't see it. Either he'd canceled last minute or was already there. Once her badge was on her dress, Rae took a moment to look around the room to see if she spotted Rob.

"Don't see him," whispered Rae as she glanced behind Flint to see if anyone else was there. She sighed in disappointment because there was no one.

"Maybe he went to the bathroom? Speaking of, didn't you have to go?"

Rae chuckled. "I was so nervous that I forgot I had to go. Is that weird? Probably. I'll be right back."

Flint nodded, and when Rae looked back, she saw that someone had already approached him. She figured he wouldn't be alone for long.

Rae found the bathroom and opened the door with ease. She walked over to the stall farthest from the door. The stall closest to the entrance was taken, and she felt awkward taking the middle one in case someone was in it. She heard someone exit the other stall, and when she was done, she opened the door and swallowed any words or sounds that she could've thought of making.

"Cassandra? What are you doing here?"

The woman at the counter looked up and smiled at Rae through the mirror. Feeling uneasy, Rae walked over to a sink that was farthest away from Cassandra Hopkins. This was the first time Rae had seen her again since Flint's mom had tried to shove her and Flint together when Flint was debating running for office. Rae put her purse on the counter and washed her hands.

"Attending the candidate meet-and-greet. I assume you are too. How have you been?"

"Okay, considering all the drama going on."

"Oh, drama. Can't live with it, can't live without it."

Rae was in the middle of drying her hands with a paper towel when she looked up at Cassandra once more. Her long, dark hair was flowing over her shoulders, and Rae assumed that the red lipstick was a trademark at this point. But what got Rae's attention was Cassandra's tone and words. It wasn't sympathetic, but more matter-of-fact. The uneasiness that she felt increased. Several things clicked in Rae's brain at once, and she went with her gut.

"How are you involved in this?"

The smile left Cassandra's face, and an expression that Rae couldn't read replaced it. "I don't know what you're talking about."

"Do you know who Edwards, Holland, and Walker Consulting or EHWC is?" She might as well just go for it.

Cassandra stood still and closed her eyes. A smirk took shape on her face before she opened her eyes. She glanced at the bathroom door before looking at Rae once more through the mirror.

"Eh. It doesn't matter at this point. I already set everything into motion, and it would be he said, she said." She rifled through her purse before she pulled out a tube of lipstick. "Yes, I know who EHWC is."

Rae adjusted her jaw as she prepared herself to ask her follow-up questions. She debated whether she could grab her phone and set it up to record without being detected, but given how Cassandra didn't take her eyes off of her, she doubted it. This might be a great time to get her to confess what she knows, but Rae thought Cassandra was right. It would be he said, she said.

"Did you hire them to dig up information on Flint and me to destroy his campaign? Did you also ransack his campaign office and leave that note along with my computer charger at my front door?"

"You're smarter than you look."

"And you are more conniving than I thought. Why? You know that you didn't have to do any of this, right?"

"Don't give me that bullshit. What's done is done, and I will continue with my plan. I have no other choice." She took out her trademark red lipstick and started applying it to her lips.

Although her words were frightening, it was the tone of her voice that sent a chill through Rae's body. That was when she knew that Cassandra had nothing to lose.

"What do you stand to gain from bringing down Flint and me?"

Cassandra stopped putting her lipstick on and thought about it. "You still don't get it, do you? I thought you were supposed to be smart." Cassandra's stare could have burnt a hole straight through Rae, but she said nothing. Cassandra huffed before she continued. "I was supposed to be in your position. On Flint's arm as he rose through the political ranks. This was the plan when we were children and was supposed to come to fruition a few years ago. But then, he met you."

Rae hoped the look on her face remained blank because she didn't want Cassandra to see how her words were affecting her. "Was he in on this? I thought you guys didn't really hang around each other."

"To be honest, I could have let everything else go. The whole me-getting-together-with-Flint thing sucked because that had been the plan for so long. But then my family's hardships spurred me to take matters into my own hands."

"Wait, a minute." Rae couldn't hold her tongue anymore. "Your family is doing fine, considering all the shit they were involved with a few months ago."

Rae jumped when Cassandra slammed her purse on the counter. "My parents have lost everything!"

Rae knew it would be better to not argue with her, but damn it, she was over this pity party. "What have they lost? Yes, they aren't making as much money, but they still have their home. Food, shelter, health, what more could you ask for?"

Cassandra's glare turned stone cold. Rae knew that she probably shouldn't be arguing with someone who had the upper hand, but this was ridiculous.

"They've been shunned from their in-circle and from their social circle at large. Their reputation is in shambles."

Rae took several deep breaths before she replied. "They

will be okay, but can you say the same for yourself? You've done a lot of damage and caused a lot of hurt. And you'll cause even more for your parents once they find out you are the one doing this. Is that what you want?"

Rae could see that her words were influencing Cassandra. Her lip trembled before she looked down at the countertop.

"I was j-just consumed by so much anger that I had to do something. I didn't want to see Flint happy. I wanted him to feel the same pain that my parents were going through."

That had done it. "That they caused! You were free to do whatever you wanted."

Cassandra straightened her stance and looked Rae in the eyes. "You still don't get it. This is what I wanted. I wanted to avenge my parents. I killed two birds with one stone because Rob will win that seat now with my help."

And that's when another point clicked in Rae's mind. "And you still get to be on the arm of a congressman. You're his plus-one today."

"Ding, ding. Speaking of, I need to head out and mingle with some folks. Maybe see you again at Rob's victory party? I'll extend a personal invitation to both you and Flint." Cassandra tossed her hair back off her shoulders, gave Rae a sickening smile, and headed toward the door. Rae tried to figure out what to do before she swung it open, but had nothing. Like she said, it was all he said, she said now. Cassandra opened the door but stopped. She slowly backed away, and it took a second before Rae could know why, and when she did, she let out the breath that she was holding in.

"Going somewhere?"

There stood Eve, holding her phone and flashing it for everyone to see.

Rae leaned on the bathroom countertop since she wasn't sure that her legs wouldn't buckle under her weight because of the relief flowing through her veins. "I don't think I've ever been so happy to see you in the entirety of our friendship."

"Doing what I can for the betterment of humanity." Eve turned to Cassandra and said, "Your ambitions are over. And she'd better hope that your boyfriend over there isn't too pissed that you pretty much ended his chance to win the primary."

Rae watched as Cassandra's head swiveled back and forth between her and Eve. Before she could do anything, Rae said, "How about we take this outside? And don't cause a scene because we don't want to detract from the main purpose of the event."

Eve nodded and led the way out of the bathroom. The three women didn't stop until they were back in the room. Rae found Flint talking two a couple of men in the spot where she left him, and as if he sensed her return, he looked up and his eyes met hers. The happiness that radiated from his facial expression quickly changed to confusion when he spotted the woman to her left. She watched as he said something to the men before he made his way over to her.

"What is going on over here?" he asked once he reached them. His eyes moved from Eve, to Cassandra, and finally to Rae, where his stare lingered. Rae realized she probably only had a short amount of time to air this out before they would attract more attention. Might as well get to the point.

"Cassandra admitted to being behind the plot to tear us down, along with your potential political career, in an effort to get revenge and propel Rob to win the primary."

"All because of the stuff our parents concocted?"

Rae saw Cassandra's face turn red before she blurted out, "You don't know what it feels like to have your life ruined."

Before either Rae or Flint could respond, Kane and Rob walked over from opposite sides of the room. This was turning into a big circus that would only attract attention, so Rae waved the group over to a more secluded corner in the room.

"Nice of you to join us, Rob. After all, you played a role in all of this as well."

Rae smirked at Rob's reaction to Flint's words. His eyes almost bulged out of his face before he caught his reaction. If that didn't tell the group he was involved and complicit, nothing would. Also, Rae concluded he would be a horrible poker player.

"We didn't—"

"Rob, save it for someone who cares. We know you were involved so drop the act. You can do the right thing now before this...leaks. We are already gaining an audience." Rae looked around and confirmed that Flint was right. People were starting to notice the group, and she figured it was only a matter of minutes before someone approached them. "The choice is up to you."

28

"I don't know why I'm nervous. Wait, that's a silly comment. I know why I'm nervous. We're going to a potential victory party, in honor of you, at your parents' house." Rae glanced down at her dress and hoped it was okay for the night's festivities. The campaign offered to throw a party together, but when Gladys West wanted to throw a fancy party for her oldest son, she got her way. Well, at least for the results of the primary, the general election would probably be a different story. Although Rae felt confident in her dress, there were nagging thoughts in the back of her mind that this still wouldn't be good enough.

Although she could have gone with another color, Rae picked a black floor-length, off-the-shoulder gown for the night's festivities. She'd asked her hairstylist to place her hair up into a chignon bun near the base of her neck and hoped the chandelier earrings that she borrowed from Jules were the perfect match for such a gown. She slipped into the strappy heels near her bedside and grabbed the evening clutch, another borrow from Jules. She walked into her living room and stopped to grab her phone off of the coffee table to see if there were any updates from Flint on when he would be arriving. Seeing nothing from him yet, Rae walked into her bathroom and gave herself one last look-over before calling Flint. She took the lip balm and the lipstick that she was planning to wear tonight and added some more color to her lips before slipping the products back into her clutch.

As her phone pinged, she hustled into her room and quickly sprayed her perfume on her neck and her wrists before returning it to its usual place on her dresser. With that, she walked back into the bathroom and grabbed her phone and checked her notifications.

Flint: *Be there in 5.*

Rae smiled as her fingers flew over the keyboard.

Rae: *I'm ready. Can't wait to see you!*

As she was placing the phone back in her clutch, she sat down on her couch to wait for Flint's arrival. A knock on the door almost five minutes later told her it was time. Rae strolled over to the door, grabbing her clutch and cover-up that she had dropped over her couch earlier that day. She looked through the peephole to confirm it was Flint, and with a deep breath, she opened the door.

Her eyes traveled down the length of Flint's body and back up before looking into his blue eyes. His body in the tux continued to reiterate that suits and tuxedos were made for Flint to wear them.

"Hello, beautiful."

"Hello, yourself. Well, now it's official."

"What's that?"

"I love you in a suit, your dress blues, and in tuxes."

Flint smirked as he ran a hand down the front of his tuxedo. "I make this tux look good, don't I?"

Rae rolled her eyes as Flint stepped back so she could close the door. When her door was locked, Flint grabbed her hand and walked her down the stairs to a black town car that was waiting for them. Once they were both in the car, the driver pulled off, starting their journey to the Wests' house.

Rae and Flint sat in comfortable silence before Flint spoke up.

"How are you doing?"

Rae thought about sugarcoating her answer before she figured telling the truth was her best bet. "I'm nervous as hell. Are you?"

"Kind of. More from an all-eyes-will-be-on-us type of thing. Like, this is it. It's do or die."

"I mean, it's not. There's still the election in November."

"Yes, but chances are the seat won't change parties then. Most predictions say whoever wins this primary, wins the seat."

Flint shrugged. "I don't want to jinx anything."

"Fair."

IT DIDN'T TAKE LONG for the couple to arrive at Flint's parents' house, and the sight of the house took Rae's breath away. Flint started walking toward the steps of his childhood home, but Rae was frozen in place. The house was the definition of stunning. The large colonial-style home with reddish-brown bricks sat on acres of land. It was lit up in a soft white light along with the driveway up to their home.

"You know, I don't think I've ever been to your parents' house," Rae said as Flint placed his hand on her lower back. Flint said nothing for a moment before he nodded his head.

"I guess you haven't. I never really thought about that, but it makes sense. We dated mostly long-distance, and then when we started dating again, my mom did everything in her power to break us up." When Rae and Flint reached the front door, Flint turned to her and asked, "Are you ready?"

"As ready as I'll ever be since I can't turn back now." He patted her back just before he opened the door and let Rae step inside before he did.

Rae was happy Flint wanted to come before the festivities began later in the evening. It gave her time to take in the house he grew up in, and it intimidated her. She assumed they had redecorated the house for the party, but she could imagine what it looked like when it was completely furnished. The interior of the home was large but homey. The warm colors on the walls to the wood floors all said classy with a capital C.

"Flint, you grew up in a beautiful home."

"Thanks. I'll have to give you a tour before everything gets started, including my childhood bedroom. I should find my parents first, though."

"That shouldn't be too hard." Both Rae and Flint turned around and smiled. Terry West greeted his son and his girlfriend with smiles. He was dressed in a tux that matched his son's, and Rae thought they resembled each other even more. Rae smirked at the glass in his hand.

Flint must have had the same train of thought because he said, "Starting the party already, old man?"

"It's never too early." Terry held up his glass and saluted

Flint before taking a sip. "Plus, your mother is running around trying to make sure that everything is set up even though I've told her a hundred times that everything is fine and to let the people we hired do their jobs. This isn't our first rodeo."

Rae watched the banter between father and son and grinned. Maybe this evening wouldn't be so bad.

"Terry, there you are. I was just talking to—" Gladys dashed into the room as fast as her shoes would allow her. Rae was shocked to find that Gladys wasn't dressed yet. Her hair and makeup looked put together, but the loose chinos and sweatshirt said differently. She stopped short with her mouth open.

"Hey, Mom."

"Flint. It's great to see you both," she said as she gestured to Rae. "Didn't expect to see you both here so soon."

"Mom, it's forty-five minutes to the fundraiser. Plus, I wanted to be here in case there were some last-minute things that needed to be done."

"Well, we need to—"

Before Gladys could launch into a to-do list, Terry sauntered over and whispered something in her ear. A light blush appeared on her cheeks before she smiled at him.

"Guys, don't worry about what else needs to be done. Everything is taken care of."

Gladys glanced at Terry before responding, "Yes, it is." She turned her attention to Rae and gave a smile. "Welcome to our home. Flint, are you planning on giving her a tour?" Flint nodded, and Gladys continued, "Great. Well, I'll finish getting ready and will be back shortly." She gave a pointed smile to her husband before ascending up the stairs.

"Dad, I don't even want to know what that was all about."

"Good, because it's none of your concern." Terry winked at his son before he headed up the stairs.

"Well, that happened," Rae said.

"Don't even ask."

"But you know what they were—"

"Babe, I don't want to think about it."

Rae laughed at Flint's objections, and it was the first time she had laughed in a while. The bundle of nerves that had been building over the last few hours was loosening. Although she was still nervous about the fundraiser itself, she didn't feel as tightly wound as she had when she arrived at the West home.

"So how about that tour?"

RAE AGREED and followed Flint down the hall. She listened as Flint showed her the various rooms of his childhood home. He opened a door and turned on a light. "So, this is your childhood bedroom." Rae took her time looking around the room as she saw into the past of the man that she was dating. "I remember you mentioned playing baseball. Didn't know you were good at it," Rae said as she eyed the trophies in his room.

"I didn't want to brag." Flint closed the door gently behind them.

She rolled her eyes and followed it up with another eye roll when she saw the smirk on his face. "Did your parents change much in your room after you went into the Air Force?" She turned her body to face his.

"Nope. Everything is exactly how I left it. Honestly, I think my mom kept my room the same in case I ever returned home. I did, briefly."

"I don't know why I fully expected your mom to have turned your room into, like, a second closet or something."

"She has one, but she probably wouldn't mind a third." The deadpan look on Flint's face made Rae laugh out. Once Rae sobered up, Flint continued. "Do you know why I brought you here?"

"To learn even more about you and what life was like for you as a child?"

"No. To get some privacy to do this." Flint took three steps and stood in front of Rae. He caressed her cheek before leaning in to kiss her. Rae's heart was about to take off when Flint broke the connection.

"Oh, shit. You're wearing lipstick."

Rae let the look of fear stay in his eyes for a few seconds before she whispered, "It's lip balm, and it can easily be wiped off and replaced. Lipstick is for when the party starts."

"You came prepared."

"Scout's honor." Rae's lips crashed into Flint's. She could feel the passion emitting from his lips as Flint placed his hand on her neck to pull her closer to him. His tongue dueled with hers to get the upper hand, and her hand moved farther south. Rae froze when they were interrupted by a knock on the door. The groan that fell from Flint's lips snapped her out of it, and she elbowed Flint in the gut after he did nothing to mask the sound.

"Yeah?" Flint answered.

"Mom is looking for you. Said she wanted to talk to you about some last-minute things before guests start arriving."

Rae immediately recognized the subtle Southern drawl that was more apparent in Flint's brother's voice than her boyfriend's.

Rae didn't move when a groan fell from Flint's lips a second time. "We'll be down in a minute." Once the footsteps faded, Flint let out a deep breath.

She smiled at him before taking a small step back. "Duty calls."

"We're picking up where that left off tonight."

"Deal."

After making sure they both looked presentable, the couple left Flint's bedroom and headed back downstairs to where the fundraiser was taking place. The Wests had turned their home into the perfect location for a party. The space was brightly lit as well, with a small set-up for microphones and speakers in the corner. In another corner sat a buffet table with white tablecloths that people were making last-minute adjustments to as they brought food out of the kitchen. A bar was set up on the other side of the room, to potentially avoid a bottleneck between the food and drinks, Rae assumed.

Rae gently swayed to the soft music until she spotted the other West children near the bar.

"While you go find your mom, I can go chat with your siblings over there."

Flint looked over to where Rae pointed and smirked. "You want to go over there because they're near the bar."

"You make that sound like it's a dreadful thing." Rae winked and turned her back on Flint as she strolled over to where his brother and twin sisters were standing.

The closer she got, the more she could hear bits and

pieces of their conversation. She was sure the twins were arguing about something and were trying to get Garrett to settle some debate they were having.

"Hey."

The twins stopped bickering long enough to turn their attention to Rae. The women greeted each other, and all talk of whatever they were debating stopped. Flint's brother gave Rae a small wave and a knowing smirk.

"What?"

"So, what were you and Flint doing in his room?"

Rae could feel her cheeks warming up, but she didn't respond before Garrett continued, "I'm kidding. I know you guys were touring the house."

"Yep. Your childhood home is beautiful." Rae hoped that that was enough to change the subject.

"It's gone through some renovations over the years, but Mom definitely put her heart and soul into making this house perfect for our family." Success.

To make matters even better, the change in subject was further cemented when the bartender came over and asked Rae what she wanted to drink. She accepted the water she requested gladly and returned her attention to Flint's siblings.

They gave Rae a brief rundown on some renovations that Gladys had done over the years, and the group had just started talking about silly things the West children had done as kids when the sound of something tinkling against glass rang throughout the room. Gladys, Terry, Flint, and Rick were standing in the entrance. Flint had been the one to gather everyone's attention and spoke first.

"I want to thank everyone who has worked very hard to

put this event together tonight. Without you, this event wouldn't be happening. I'll save the rest of my thanks for another moment tonight but wanted to catch everyone who was working hard behind the scenes to make sure tonight is a success. Thank you."

The staffers said their thank-yous and your-welcomes before going back to finishing the tasks they were working on. Rae continued to watch Flint as he turned his attention to Rick and Kate, who Rae hadn't noticed was behind Rick while Flint was speaking. The discussion looked to be pretty serious, based on Flint's expressions. She thought about going over there to talk to him but didn't want to disrupt anything related to his campaign. Rae turned her attention back to his siblings and rejoined their conversation.

It was only a short time later that the party began and guests arrived. About an hour into the event, Rae didn't know how many people she had met by that point, but making small talk with other guests at the fundraiser was exhausting. Rae found herself near the bar once again and decided that now was the time to spice up her drink choice a bit and ordered some red wine.

As she was waiting, she felt a tap on her shoulder.

"What are you all doing here?!"

Jules, Liv, and Eve smiled back at their friend before Eve replied, "We wouldn't miss this for the world but thought we'd surprise you. How is everything going?"

Rae thanked the bartender for her wine before giving her girlfriends her full attention. "Everything is going well, I think. I've talked to way too many people to count, and thankfully no one has brought up the picture or any of the drama surrounding Cassandra and Rob."

"That's good. I know you were concerned about it."

"Still am, to be honest. But at least Cassandra fessed up to what she did. I'm actually somewhat happy that Rob didn't drop out of the race."

"Why is that?" Liv asked as she lifted the glass of wine and mouthed *thank you* at a server who brought the group a drink before turning her attention back to Rae.

"'Cause everyone else wasn't gaining traction, and I didn't want there to be an asterisk next to Flint's name saying that he only won because Rob dropped out."

"That's legit."

"Well, hello there."

The women turned to the person who interrupted their conversation. Jules rolled her eyes before she said, "Garrett."

"When you say my name like that, it hurts my heart."

"Get real and get over yourself." This time, Jules's words came out as a whisper. Rae was amazed at her ability to be stern, but in a way that made it seem that the conversation at hand was pleasant.

"I just came over here to say hi."

"You've said it, and now you can leave."

Rae, Liv, and Eve looked back and forth between the two, stunned. Rae knew she should probably try to defuse the situation, but the words weren't forming to attempt to stop the train wreck.

"Listen, Jules, I know—"

"Not right now, Garrett. Okay?" Rae noticed the change in Jules's tone, as it almost became like a plea to get him to leave her alone.

"Fine. I'll see you around." With one long, lingering glance, Garrett went on his way.

"What the hell was that all about? And why didn't you mention that you had history with Flint's brother?"

"Honestly? It's something I wanted to leave in the past. We were...young. I'll tell you all about it sometime, but right now is definitely not the place or time." She glanced in the direction Garrett walked in and said, "I didn't know he was back in town, and I wish he wasn't."

Rae nodded her head. "These West men are something else." She made a mental note to ask Flint if he knew anything about Jules's history with his brother.

Jules snorted in response, which made Rae look her way. Jules was usually the most "proper" of their group, so to see her not give a damn, especially in public, was a sight to see.

"You can say that again."

THE PARTY CONTINUED, and with the help of Jules, Rae could identify who were some of the most important people in the room. If she ended up speaking to them, she tried to put her best foot forward. Thinking she needed a breather, Rae slipped out a side door and onto the patio overlooking the Wests' backyard. Being outside, away from the crowd, gave her a sense of tranquility. She could take in some deep breaths of fresh air and relieve some anxiety she had been feeling in that house full of people.

A few moments later, she felt a hand on the small of her back and turned to smile at her boyfriend. "Haven't seen you most of the night."

"I know, and I'm sorry about that. It's been—"

Rae smiled at Flint. "I didn't mean that was a bad thing. I know you're busy talking to folks and everything." She looked around the garden before looking back to the party and said, "Things seem to be going well."

"Yeah, I can't complain. Are you enjoying tonight?"

Rae nodded her head just before her eyes grew wide. "Flint, do you know anything about something happening between Jules and Garrett?"

Flint didn't respond right away. When he did, he shook his head. "No. I know they were in the same grade in elementary school and high school. Plus, she is great friends with the twins because they were in a lot of the same extracurricular activities. Why? Did something happen?"

Rae told Flint about the interaction between Garrett and Jules and watched the smirk form on his lips.

"Interesting. Yeah, I don't know what might have caused that, but it might have been after I left home. I'll find out more about it when I have a chance."

"Sounds like a great plan." Rae reached up and planted a small peck on his lips. "Thought I should do that now before someone steals you away from me again."

"Yeah, we should probably get back in there. Ready, m'lady?" He held out his arm for her to take.

"Oh, yes. Thank you, kind sir." Rae curtsied, and Flint chuckled before he escorted her back into the West family home.

Once they were back in the event space, Rae looked around to see who she should talk to next, and her eyes landed on someone she hadn't expected to see. The gasp that left her lips led Flint to ask, "Are you okay?"

"Yeah. Look who's talking to your parents. Near the window closest to the front door." Flint swung his head and found who Rae was talking about.

"Calvin and Marie Hopkins. You've got to be kidding me."

"Are you shocked they're here? I'm not. A) it's a party, b) they are trying to win over their former friends again, and c) they're probably trying to smooth over the crap their daughter caused."

"Should we go say something? Chances are you won't be able to make it over there with everyone wanting to talk to you." Rae turned and looked at Flint as she lowered her voice to make sure that the people surrounding them couldn't hear.

Flint's eyes were still fixed on the scene across the room. "Looks like we don't have to make that decision. They're on their way over here now."

With that, Rae turned her attention back to the Wests and Hopkinses, and Flint was right. Gladys waved her hand briefly, letting Flint know that they were coming to them as the two couples were making their way across the room. She wasn't over all the mayhem that they and Gladys had caused. Hell, she didn't know if she would ever be over it.

The first person to speak when the couples arrived was Gladys.

"Flint, Rae, look who surprised us and showed up at the fundraiser." Although Rae said nothing, she had some questions about how much of a surprise this was, especially with an airtight guest list.

"It's nice to see you again," Rae said with gritted teeth. It took everything in her to not roll her eyes at how effortlessly the lie rolled off her tongue. She spared a glance over at Flint after she noticed he hadn't said anything. His expression was blank.

"It's great to see you again. We just wanted to come out and support Flint in any way we can." Rae's eyes cut over to Marie's. She couldn't control the glare that she knew was coming from her. "We also wanted to apologize once again."

Marie said the last few words so quietly that Rae wasn't sure she heard them correctly. When no one else said anything, Calvin chimed in, "We shouldn't have done what we did. We took things too far. You both deserve to be happy, and if that's with one another, then that's how it should be."

Rae saw that Flint gave them a small nod out of the corner of her eye. *I bet they are trying to make nice with him because he has a fantastic chance of winning the primary. Better to be on the winning ticket from the start than hop on closer to the end.*

"Well…" Rae smiled internally because neither Flint nor she were giving them anything to work with. "If you need anything else, please let us know."

Flint gave another small nod before saying, "Cool. I have to get back to talking to my guests." And with that, Flint slipped his hand around Rae's and started making his way through the crowd. Once he was far enough away from the scene, he turned back to look at Rae before she spoke.

"I understand why you needed to get us out of there, but you couldn't have pulled us in the bar's direction?"

Rae's question led to a slight smile appearing on Flint's lips. Her attempt at trying to take his mind off of the encounter had worked.

"That would have been a smarter decision. Tried to find your friends instead before I had to step up and make a speech that Rick keeps signaling me is time to make." Rae looked up. There were Jules, Liv, and Eve a few feet away, and she looked to her left and saw that Rick was looking at them as he walked over.

"That was kind of amazing."

"I know." By the time Flint responded, they were near her friends, who glanced up just before the duo got to them. Flint greeted them all with a brief hug before turning to Rae. "I'll see you after my speech, okay?" Rae nodded, and Flint gave her a small peck before walking away.

Rae stood off to the side as she watched Flint take the stage. She glanced to her left when she felt someone's presence enter her personal space. The person she saw caused her to tilt her head back and look up at the ceiling.

"Rick." She had forgotten all about him in those brief thirty seconds.

"Rae." Rick adjusted his tie and nodded his head toward the stage. "He looks good."

"That's not surprising." Growing bored with this small talk, Rae cleared her throat and whispered, "I'm no longer pretending that I'm someone I'm not. If anyone has a problem with it, they can deal with it. Including you."

Rick swallowed hard and pulled on his suit jacket to straighten it. Rae could see that her words hit their mark. "I was only trying to ensure that Flint had the best chance at winning the primary."

"And I have the same goal. But not to the detriment of myself. If that's not good enough, then you can take it up with Flint, the person who hired you." Rae spared Rick one last glare before she gave him a smile and shifted away from him. She wasn't going to let him ruin her day. She could feel his eyes on her before he turned around and focused on his client.

Rae walked over to where her friends were, closer to the stage, and watched the speeches unfold.

❧

"Are you excited to watch this?" Jules whispered as Terry was trying to get the crowd's attention.

"Nervous for him. I always get a rush when he talks in front of a group of people, especially about what he's passionate about. Doesn't make me any less nervous for him, though, because I know he is putting everything he has into this and more." Rae sighed. "I'm worried that all of this will be for naught if he loses tonight."

Before Jules could respond, Terry started speaking. He didn't hold back on the praises and love that he showed his oldest son. Rae could tell that he meant every word he said, and they made her emotional. The love he had for his son was as clear as day and made her think about the relationship that she had with her own parents.

As Terry wrapped up his introduction, Rae glanced at Gladys, who was standing off just to the left of her husband. She dabbed her eyes with a napkin before taking her turn at the microphone. She repeated a few of the same things her husband mentioned before, but also shared some quick stories about Flint when he was growing up and how she always knew that he would strive to achieve any goal that he set for himself. Once she wrapped her speech, she introduced Flint to the people who supported him. The crowd went wild when Flint stepped up to the microphone. Once the crowd quieted down, Flint began his speech.

"Thank you, everyone, for coming out tonight. Hopefully, I'll be back up here in a few when the results come in that we are continuing on 'til November!" The guests went clapped loudly once more.

"I want to first start out by thanking my parents for putting together this wonderful party and hosting it in their home. Without you, this wouldn't have happened." The crowd gave a round of applause to Terry and Gladys. "To my siblings, Garrett, Allie, and Lily, thanks for putting up with me and for being here to support me tonight." While the audience clapped for them, the trio did a small wave in acknowledgment of the praise. "To my team, you guys have been doing a wonderful job, and I couldn't ask for a better group of people to work with. Thanks so much for all the hard work you've been doing so we can make it to the finish line." Rick and Kate, representing Team West, mouthed their thanks as the crowd clapped once again.

"And to the love of my life." Rae could see Flint briefly look through the crowd until his eyes met Rae's. The butterflies in her stomach soared to new heights as all eyes turned to her as the crowd continued their thunderous applause. "Wait, this isn't right. Rae, can you please come up here?" Rae paused for a second before she made her way up to where Flint was standing. She could feel his eyes on her, and when she was a couple of feet away, he held his hand out for her to grab, and once she placed her hand in his, he squeezed it gently.

"Thanks for being here with me every step of the way. This road hasn't been easy, and I wouldn't have made it without you by my side. I love you." He gave her a polite kiss on the cheek that reminded her of his promise for later. She refrained from fanning her face, although it was growing warmer due to his words and everyone staring at her.

"Feel free to continue drinking and eating, and hopefully we will have something to celebrate tonight." The applause thundered through the house as Flint and Rae left the microphone. They both received smiles and hugs as the two walked over to where Rae's friends were. All of the Wests soon joined them with Kane, who had just arrived.

"Better late than never," Flint said as he shook Kane's hand.

"I had to finish something up that took longer than

planned." Kane greeted the entire group and somehow ended up next to Eve, who side-eyed him, but said nothing. Before Rae could say something snarky about Jules and Eve having to deal with men they didn't like, Rick and another person walked up to the stage as a projector, and a screen came down from the ceiling.

"Another addition that my parents made about a year ago," Flint whispered to Rae as the setup continued.

Once everything was ready, the two headed down, and Rae smirked as Kate handed Rick another drink. She assumed someone was nervous.

The whole room watched in silence as the results trickled in.

"Holy shit, you're starting to pull away," Rae whispered to Flint, whose eyes hadn't moved from the screen. The only signal that she received that he had heard her talking to him was the slight squeeze he once again gave her hand.

Flint continued to pull away. Once it was projected that Flint had won the primary, the crowd cheered. Flint grabbed Rae and hoisted her into the air as she whispered to him, "You did it."

"Babe, we did this." His lips ended up on hers, and they didn't care who was watching. Flint waved from his position in the crowd, acknowledging and thanking everyone for all of their support. He hugged Rae again before going down the line and hugging his family and then heading back up to the microphone.

"We did it!" Flint's shout with glee pumped up the crowd once more while they gave him a standing ovation. Flint continued his celebratory speech as Rae looked around the room and watched the looks on everyone's faces. Even the

Hopkinses looked pleased that Flint had won the primary. When Rae turned her attention back to Flint, she let out a gigantic sigh of relief. The mess that had been the race to win the primary was over.

"Doing okay over there?"

Rae turned her attention to Eve, who was now standing next to her. "I'm doing amazingly well."

A few months later, Rae waved at the security guard sitting behind the front desk. She waited patiently while he pressed a button that opened the heavy glass door. She walked inside, her heels clicking on the floor as she walked to the front desk.

"Hi. I'm hoping to see Flint West."

"Is he expecting you?" the security guard asked as he reached for the office phone—a valid question since it was after work hours.

"No, he doesn't know I'm here, but I can call him to confirm if that makes things easier. I was hoping to surprise him if that was possible. I'm his girlfriend."

The security guard gave her a slight smile before he said, "Let me call up to confirm that he's in, but I won't tell him you're here. Please, just sign here, and I'll quickly print out a badge." He held the office phone in one hand as he typed on the keyboard with his other.

"Hi, Mr. West? I know, I know. I keep forgetting to call you Flint. I apologize. I have some documents that have just been delivered that I can bring up to you." He paused for a moment. "Sure, I'll be up in a minute." He paused again. "You're welcome."

It took about a minute for Rae and the security guard to wrap up the signing-in process, but in no time, she was thanking the security guard for his help and walking over to the elevators. Her excitement built once she was on the elevator as she watched the numbers increase. She was getting closer and closer to seeing the love of her life, someone she hadn't been able to spend as much time with as of late because of busy schedules. That was potentially ending tonight. If worse came to worst, she brought her laptop and could do some tasks for her job, which she was now back to working full time, while she waited for him to finish up whatever he was doing. Either way, they would be together, and that was what mattered to her.

When the elevator arrived at Flint's floor, she took a deep breath and waited for the doors to open. Once they did, she stepped off the elevator and headed toward the front desk of the law firm. Noticeably absent was Brooke, who usually sat at the front desk to welcome visitors. She looked around the office space and was shocked to see it deserted, but maybe that was her own assumptions that made her think that was the case. Rae silently thanked whoever designed their office space because they had left carpet in, quietening her footsteps as she walked toward Flint's office. She slowed her pace down just before she got to Flint's door.

Rae did her best to pat down her hair before she turned the corner and stood in the doorway of Flint's office. He must have been so engrossed in something he was reading because he didn't look up, even though she figured he would have normally seen her out of the corner of his eye.

"Special delivery, Mr. Future Congressman." Although she cringed inwardly at her comment, Flint didn't laugh at her after the words left her mouth. She saw a brief look of surprise that appeared on his face that shifted in a flash and was replaced with a smile as he placed the pen he was holding down and stood up.

"What are you doing here? Are you the documents that were supposedly delivered to the front desk?"

"I am. I wanted to see you, and I know how busy your schedule is, so I figured if we couldn't hang out outside of work, why don't I just bring my work with me, and we can do it together?"

Rae's eyes didn't veer off of Flint as he walked over to her and brushed a strand of hair off of her shoulder. He leaned down and whispered, "I think that's an excellent idea." He placed a small kiss in the crook of her neck.

When his hands started drifting toward her neck where she assumed he thought her zipper was, she spoke. "Zipper's not there, and aren't you concerned that someone might walk in on us?"

Flint took a step back and nodded. "You know what? You're right."

Rae smiled. "You know I'll never tire of hearing you say that."

She watched as Flint walked around her and locked his office door. He then pulled the blinds down that blocked the little window next to the door so no one who walked by could see in. He walked past Rae once more while he undid the cuffs on his shirt and rolled the sleeves up his forearms. He went over to his office windows and lowered the blinds there too. The only light illuminating the room was a small lamp on his desk. He walked over to his desk and stood behind it with one hand in his pocket. His gaze was trained on Rae.

"I thought I came here to work with you?" Rae's words came out with a slight quiver, which she was sure didn't go unnoticed by Flint.

"Oh, I have something to work out, but I don't think we're talking about the same thing."

Rae couldn't stop the sly smile that appeared on her face. She bit her lip, and Flint's stare went from her eyes down to her mouth.

"I do have some things I need to complete for work. Plus, I'm a little nervous that someone might watch us and is just waiting to leak photos of us being intimate."

Rae knew right away on the one hand she shouldn't have said those words. On the other hand, she did what she thought was best for Flint and his career in politics. And with that, she might have just opened up Pandora's box.

"Is that always in the back of your mind? Before we have sex?"

"No, of course not."

"Well, Cassandra, Sarah, and Rob are all out of the picture, this building and this office are very secure, and no one is around. So why don't we have a little fun? After all, our anniversary is in a few days, and we can celebrate early."

Before Rae could utter a response, Flint's lips were on hers, kissing her senseless. She felt Flint's hands move down her body before touching her butt. The next thing she knew, she was being lifted to the desk, and neither one of them cared what had fallen to the floor. By the time Rae was sitting on the desk, her dress had been pushed up to her thighs, making it easy for Flint to step between her legs.

"Flint," Rae sighed as she tried to get Flint even closer to her. His kisses moved down to her neck, to the spot he knew would drive her to the brink. She could feel him trying to feel around once more to find the zipper to her dress, but he was still unsuccessful.

"This might be the worst dress you own." Rae barely heard Flint's words that he murmured into her neck.

"Why is that?"

"Because I can't figure out how to get it off."

Rae chuckled and moved her arms that had been holding on to Flint. She grabbed hold of her dress's fabric in one hand and maneuvered her other hand to grab the zipper and unzipped the dress herself. Flint then helped her lift the dress over her head.

"Do me a favor and burn this dress, okay?" As he was about to lean in to kiss her again, he did a double-take. "Is this new?"

Rae nodded. "I might have had a little time to do some lingerie shopping a week ago. Thought today was a good a day as any to try it on. Changed into it when I got home before heading over here." She gestured to the navy blue bra and panty set she was wearing. While she was speaking, he pulled his shirt out of his slacks and unbuttoned it.

"Excellent decision. Too bad it's going to end up on the floor." With ease, Flint unsnapped her bra and placed his palms over her breasts. He ran his fingers over her nipples, alternating between softly caressing them and pinching them. His lips returned to that spot on her neck, and the only thing she could hear was her moans and his kisses. Rae's head fell back, giving Flint even better access to her neck. His kisses moved down her body and to her breast, where he then put one nipple in his mouth while continuing to alternate between caressing and pinching the other.

He slid down her body and stared at the dark blue panties. "You know, maybe these can stay on for the time being." He pushed the light fabric to the side before he began playing where she wanted him most. His fingers worked her into a frenzy, and in one swift motion, he had her body lying face-down on his desk. Her eyes wandered around parts of his office that she could see from this position and landed on a photo of them from one of the trips she had taken to visit him on base. She studied it as she heard him unbuckling his pants and opening the condom. Rae smiled at the memory before groaning when he slid into her.

"Yes!" was the only thing Rae said as Flint found a rhythm that would mean it was only a matter of time before he brought them the pleasure they craved. Rae's body buckled even before Flint collapsed on her top of her as his motions slowed down. She was still shuddering when he caught his breath and removed himself from her.

"My brain is completely scrambled."

Rae just made random noises in response, leading Flint to chuckle.

"How about we help pull each other together, clean up, and head to your apartment to continue this celebration?" All Rae did was nod before laying her head back down on the table.

EPILOGUE

"**Y**ou know, even with movers, moving sucks," Rae said as she opened yet another box of the things they brought into the house. The sun was setting, casting a warm glow inside the new home they were now renting.

"I think the world would agree with you."

"You know what sucks more?"

"What's that?"

"Moving just before you were planning to go on vacation." Rae's last move had been hellish when she scheduled it too close to her organization's board meeting. Having the moving company cancel last minute didn't help either. She thought about when Flint helped save her move, and although she wouldn't have admitted it at the time, she was grateful.

"You're not wrong," said Flint. "Where do you want this?"

Rae turned her head to look at Flint. "That should go in the bedroom...it should be written on the box." She walked over to him and pointed at the word *Bedroom* on the box. She had also placed a bright yellow piece of duct tape on it, dictating its location if someone needed to reference the moving chart she created a couple of days ago.

"What's in here? Feels somewhat light," Flint said as he adjusted his hold the box.

Rae examined to box for a second before a smile appeared on her face. "That's for me to know and for you to find out at some point, Mr. Congressman." She was sure that was the box where she stuck her lingerie and other bedroom items. Flint had won the general election a week ago, and the couple heard they could officially move into this house a day later. Thankfully, they had already started packing their things, under the impression that the house would be their new home, and the only holdup was paperwork.

Flint raised an eyebrow at her before giving her a kiss on the cheek and walking up the stairs, heading to what she assumed was their new bedroom. Although it was a bigger hassle for them both to move versus having her move in with him at his old apartment, the move allowed him to be closer to the Hill, while not making her commute horrible.

Rae went into their kitchen and continued unpacking the boxes the movers had placed in there earlier. Once she placed all the items in a place that she liked, she brushed her hands on her yoga pants covered thighs, and took a step back. Just as she was confirming whether she liked the items in their current locations, Flint called her from the bedroom.

"Babe?"

"Yeah?" Rae said as she walked closer to the bedroom door.

"Could you go out to my car and grab my tools? I left my keys on one of the boxes near the door."

She wondered why he couldn't grab his keys himself but said nothing as she walked farther down the hall to the front door. She glanced around the house in amazement. They were really renting this house. The three-bedroom house allowed them to turn one bedroom into a guest room in case they had any out-of-town visitors, and the other bedroom could be an office. It was big enough for them to share the space if it came down to that. What had sold Rae on the house was the kitchen. Although the kitchen at Flint's apartment had been great, this kitchen allowed them to have more room to maneuver around in and host small get-togethers without a problem. It also didn't hurt that they now had a backyard that allowed for them to potentially get a dog soon. If Flint would go along with it.

She headed outside, closed the front door, and walked down the three steps before taking a right toward the driveway where her and Flint's cars were parked. She pressed a button, and the trunk of his sedan popped open. Rae guessed the tools might have been there, but quickly proved herself wrong. She closed the trunk with a thud before pressing another button twice on the remote and opening up the back seat on the passenger's side.

After moving around some odds and ends that had been left over from their move, she still couldn't find the tools. "Dude, did you forget where you put them?" she asked as she opened the passenger's side door. Once again, there was nothing there.

Thinking Flint must have lost his mind, she almost closed the car door when she noticed a yellow Post-it note on the glove compartment. She picked it up before shaking her head.

Sorry. :-)

Rae closed the car door and pressed the lock button on the car remote before heading toward the front door of her new home. She jogged up the steps on the porch, opened her front door once more, and entered the home.

"Flint?" she called as she headed toward the stairs. No response greeted her.

"Flint," she said again, her patience wearing thin. "This isn't funny." She played with the necklace he gave her months months ago as she searched for him.

Once again, he didn't respond, which further raised alarm bells in her head. Was this his attempt to scare her? But the note didn't sound scary. She walked down the hallway toward the stairs as she tried to figure out why Flint wanted her out of the house. Once she reached the top of the stairs, she could see that the bedroom door was closed. With a little more pep in her step, she marched over to the bedroom door and turned the knob.

As she pushed the door open, she let out a gasp, and her hands raced to her face, covering her mouth. The room was lit up with candles and on the floor lay red roses mixed in with what looked to be purple flowers, reminding of when he first bought her those flowers for their first official date years ago. The best thing of all was that Flint was down on one knee with an enormous smile on his face.

"I always hoped I would get the opportunity to propose to you. Even when we broke up years ago. I knew you were it for me. I thought about how I wanted to do it, but nothing seemed like the right opportunity until now. Rae, you are the light of my life, and nothing in this life would mean anything without you in mine. Forever. Will you marry me?"

"Yes! Of course, I will. I can't believe you did this!" Rae darted over to Flint and kneeled down in front of him before crashing into his arms. She leaned back briefly before her lips landed on his. The sensual kiss was halted when Rae realized she was crying and pulled away.

"How? When? What?" she asked as she tried to wipe the tears from her eyes.

"How about I put this ring on your finger first, and then we can talk about everything?"

Rae shook her head. "Holy shit, I didn't even get an opportunity to look at it yet."

Flint chuckled as he slid the ring onto her left hand. Rae's eyes grew wide.

"This is the ring I wanted! How did you...?" Rae's words trailed off as she was stunned into silence. She looked up at Flint and leaned forward to hug him again. When she pulled away this time, Flint stood up and helped her up with him.

"Getting a little too old to be on your knees for lengthy periods of time?"

"That isn't what you said a couple of nights ago. In fact, I think it was—" Before Flint could finish the rest of his sentence, Rae lightly elbowed him, causing him to chuckle once more. "Okay, okay. How about we walk downstairs to the kitchen and grab some champagne to celebrate?"

"Champagne? I thought that was just to christen us starting our new 'living together' journey. Brilliant," Rae said as she blew out the candles in the room.

"I can be clever sometimes." Flint joined her in picking up the remnants of their celebration. Rae saw him stop out of the corner of her eye and come over to her once they finished picking up the candles.

"I'll take care of the petals later. Let's go have some champagne."

The couple made their way downstairs and into the kitchen. Flint opened the champagne while Rae went to grab a pair of flutes.

"Who would have thought these would have come in handy when Liv gave them to me a few years back?" Liv had given the flutes to Rae when the hotel she worked for was getting rid of their old china.

Flint laughed before handing Rae the bottle of champagne while he strolled back over to the fridge. He came back with an assortment of snacks, and once Rae had the flutes, they walked into the living room, which was the most put-together room in the house so far because Flint had insisted on hooking up the television as soon as possible.

"So how did you do...well, everything?"

Flint smirked and replied, "Your mom, Liv, Eve, and Jules helped me with the ring."

"That makes sense. It was either that, or you were creeping through my search history. Also makes sense because I don't think I ever talked to you about what type of ring I wanted?" Rae paused and studied the ring; it felt like a foreign object, yet she never wanted to take it off. "How long have you had it?"

"A few weeks now. I had it made and then picked it up on the way to a campaign event. Actually, it was one of the events you attended with me, and you were wondering why I seemed a bit...off."

"Well, now I know why."

Flint grabbed her hand and, with his finger, twisted the ring back and forth. When he stopped, he looked into her eyes and confirmed, "Yes, now you know why." He leaned in to kiss her, and just before their kissing turned it to a full-blown make out session, Rae pulled away, placing her hands on his chest.

"We need to tell our families and friends that we're engaged."

"True. How do you want to do that?"

"Well, we can do video calls and let them know."

Flint looked at Rae suspiciously. "Why do I think that's not the route you want to take?"

Rae smiled. "Because you know me too well. I might have an idea."

"You know we are late to our own engagement celebration party...that no one knows is happening, right?" Flint asked as he and Rae rushed down the street.

"I know, I know. It took me longer than planned to get off the phone with Danielle and finish up some last-minute things from work. Holy crap, it's cold out here," she said as the wind picked up a bit. She tried to snuggle deeper into her winter coat as Flint wrapped an arm around her. He rubbed his hand up and down her shoulder, and when she looked up at him, she found him smiling at her. He turned away as the two hurried down the street. They were on their way to the Green Hat to greet their friends and family under the guise of wanting to celebrate Flint's victory. What they didn't know was that Rae and Flint had another surprise to share.

A few minutes later, the couple arrived at the bar, and Flint held open the door as Rae walked in. Liv had volunteered to be the point person to help organize this little shindig with John, the owner of the Green Hat. Luckily, Liv hadn't asked too many questions about what the event was for and had been happy to put it together.

Rae and Flint were greeted with a round of applause when they walked into one of the closed-off section of the bar that the Green Hat had designated for private parties. Rae let Flint help her out of her coat after he put his on the coat rack near the entrance to the room. Once the two were settled, Flint cleared his throat as Rae kept her left hand hidden from view.

"First, I want to thank everyone for coming. I know this was last minute since Rae and I are leaving to go on vacation in a couple of days."

"It's about time!" Liv said, interrupting Flint's speech. The crowd laughed at Liv's outburst as Flint shook his head. Rae took a moment to look at her parents, her friends, Flint's family, Kane, and some of their other friends, some of his campaign staff, and some of his soon-to-be congressional staffers.

Once the room quieted down, Flint continued. "Second, I'm sure a few of you would agree that this is also 'about time.'" Flint looked down at Rae.

"We're engaged!" With that, Rae readjusted herself, pulling out her hand that had been tucked into Flint's side almost since they had arrived. The first shout she heard was from her mother, whose face was now being covered by hands and buried into her father's chest. She watched her father give Flint a knowing smile before turning his attention to his daughter.

Rae dashed over to her parents, and Stella looked up a

few seconds before her daughter was in front of her. She and Jake pulled their only child into a hug that lasted for several moments. When Rae took a step back, she looked up at her dad and asked, "Did you two know anything about this?"

"We might have." Stella reached over and tapped her husband on the shoulder. "What's funny is that your mother knew this was coming."

"I knew that it was coming. I didn't know *when* it was coming. I didn't expect it to be so soon after the election. Not that I'm not happy about it. Oh, Rae, I'm so happy for you!" Stella leaned over to give Rae another hug.

As the hug broke apart, Rae asked, "When did Flint talk to you about us getting married?"

Stella looked up at Jake before looking back at her daughter. "I think it was a couple of months back." Stella shook her head before she continued, "Time seems to be flying by. Yes, it had to be a couple of months ago. You were out with your girlfriends at happy hour, and he took us out to dinner to talk about it. He made it clear that he wanted to let us know this is something you two both wanted, and he hoped we were happy with your decision. And to say we are thrilled is an understatement. I love you so much, baby."

Stella looked down at the ring before she leaned in again to give Rae another hug. Rae felt her father place his hand on her back, and she assumed he had placed his other hand on his wife's. Stella leaned back and tried to contain her tears with her fingers. "I told myself I wouldn't cry when this happened and look at me. Almost a bumbling mess."

Rae shook her head as she watched her father comfort her mother. She heard some squealing behind her and turned around to find her three best friends standing in the middle of the room. Her friends ran to her side and gave her an enormous bear hug.

"He proposed! He finally did it!"

The excited comments from the women all came out in a rush, and Rae couldn't keep up. "Hey, guys, slow down. I can't understand a thing you're saying."

Liv was the first one to let the words flow from her lips. "You could have told me I was planning an engagement party!?"

Rae giggled before she said, "I know, but where's the fun in that? Besides, we aren't sure if we really want to do all of that, anyway. If we do, it'll be at a later date, and I promise I'll let you plan it and be completely in the know. Okay?"

Liv nodded her head, completely satisfied with that answer. "Now on to more important news. You're engaged!"

Rae nodded her head as she couldn't stop the smile from appearing on her face.

"Well, let's see the ring," demanded Eve as she held out her hand, waiting for Rae to place it in hers. The women took a long look at the ring and oohed and aahed.

Jules reached over and gave Rae another hug. "I can't believe you're going to be a married woman soon."

"Well, not too soon. We haven't discussed anything about a wedding date or even a wedding."

"How'd he pop the question?"

Rae gave her friends a rundown of how Flint proposed to her and how she concluded that getting all of their loved ones together at the Green Hat was the cherry on top.

"So now you need to tell me how Flint knew exactly what design I wanted."

"Well, at first, he wanted to make time to meet us all for

lunch, but none of our schedules could line up. So we had a video chat where we showed him some designs you liked, and he took it from there." Eve gave Rae a big grin after she finished telling what she knew.

"Yeah, when did this happen? Wasn't it right around the time we found out about Sarah?"

Liv and Jules nodded but said nothing. Rae refused to go down that path again. This was a time to celebrate, not a time to be upset.

Rae looked to the other side of the room and saw Gladys, Terry, and Flint talking to each other. Gladys's eyes met Rae's, and she gave her a small smile. Rae excused herself from her friends and made her way over to her future husband and in-laws.

"Congrats to you both!" Terry exclaimed when Rae appeared at Flint's side. Flint, whose back was to her when she arrived, turned around and gave his fiancée a kiss on the cheek and wrapped an arm around her waist.

"I'm so happy for you guys."

Rae gave Gladys a smile after her kind words.

"Thank you so much," Rae replied. And she truly meant it.

"Is it all right if I give you a hug?" Rae appreciated her asking, especially given how shaky their relationship was in the past. She nodded, and the two embraced. Rae felt as if this hug was her way of telling herself that it was okay to forgive Gladys. Now, she'll never forget what happened, but she also didn't want to hold a grudge in this case.

Rae took a step back and gave Gladys a small smile. She then hugged Terry before Flint and she made their way around the room to greet the rest of their guests. Once they made the rounds, Flint gestured toward the entrance of the room with his head and led Rae out of their private party room.

"Is everything okay?" Rae asked when he stopped. The two found themselves standing in front of another bar just outside of the private area they had rented.

"Yeah. Just wanted to take a breather. There has been a lot of excitement over the last couple of weeks."

"That's an understatement. In fact, I would wager there has been a lot of excitement since we started dating again."

Flint nodded his head before saying, "That's an accurate assessment." He laughed, and Rae followed suit. "I wouldn't want to be on this journey with anyone else."

"You know what's funny?" Flint raised an eyebrow at her, waiting to see where she was going with this. "Neither would I."

Flint playfully rolled his eyes and leaned down to kiss the joke away.

ABOUT THE AUTHOR

B. Ivy Woods has been writing for as long as she can remember. After getting her Bachelor of Arts in Political Science and Environmental Policy and a Master's in Energy Policy and Law degree and working in the environmental field for several years, she decided to become a stay-at-home mom. That is when thoughts of a writing career really took off. Although she competed in NaNoWriMo multiple times, 2019 was the first year that she won. This win inspired her to make writing a career. Her debut novel was self-published in 2020.

Although she is originally from New York City, she currently lives in the DMV (Washington, D.C., Maryland, Virginia) with her husband, daughter, dog, and cat.

www.bivywoods.com